(3.0)

The Phantom Pass

Also by William Colt MacDonald in Large Print:

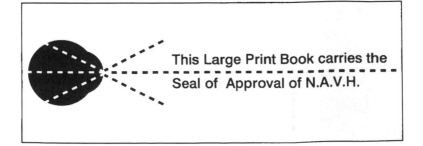

This Large Print Book carries the
Seal of Approval of N.A.V.H.

The Phantom Pass

William Colt MacDonald

WHEELER
PUBLISHING

Published in 2003 by arrangement with
Golden West Literary Agency.

Wheeler Large Print Western Series.

The text of this Large Print edition is unabridged.
Other aspects of the book may vary from the original edition.

Set in 16 pt. Plantin by Minnie B. Raven.

Printed in the United States on permanent paper.

Library of Congress Cataloging-in-Publication Data

MacDonald, William Colt, 1891–1968.
    [Punchers of Phantom Pass]
    The Phantom Pass / William Colt MacDonald.
      p. cm.
    Originally published: Punchers of Phantom Pass. London :
Collins, 1939.
    ISBN 1-58724-470-5 (lg. print : sc : alk. paper)
    1. Large type books.   I. Title.
PS3525.A2122P86 2003
813'.52—dc21   2003052520

The Phantom Pass

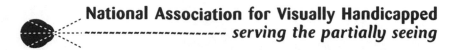

National Association for Visually Handicapped
------------------------- *serving the partially seeing*

As the Founder/CEO of NAVH, the only national health agency solely devoted to those who, although not totally blind, have an eye disease which could lead to serious visual impairment, I am pleased to recognize Thorndike Press★ as one of the leading publishers in the large print field.

Founded in 1954 in San Francisco to prepare large print textbooks for partially seeing children, NAVH became the pioneer and standard setting agency in the preparation of large type.

Today, those publishers who meet our standards carry the prestigious "Seal of Approval" indicating high quality large print. We are delighted that Thorndike Press is one of the publishers whose titles meet these standards. We are also pleased to recognize the significant contribution Thorndike Press is making in this important and growing field.

Lorraine H. Marchi, L.H.D.
Founder/CEO
NAVH

★ Thorndike Press encompasses the following imprints: Thorndike, Wheeler, Walker and Large Pr int Press.

1. Winter on the Beartrap

It had been a hard winter on the Beartrap outfit that year. The wolves had accounted for a good many head of stock, and coyotes hadn't been slow to take care of the stray cattle the lobos had overlooked. The ravines and gullies were piled deeply with drifted snow, and, although the stronger cows managed to forage for themselves and located sparse bits of old grass on the higher spots, the majority of cattle ribs were commencing to stand out in alarming fashion. Another thing that bothered Tuck Samson, owner of the Beartrap Ranch, was the fact that hay for the weaklings was disappearing fast from his barns.

This matter of insufficient hay, though, was largely Samson's own fault. He hadn't put up enough to get through the winter. That was Samson — for the sake of saving a few dollars he'd take a chance on the winter being short and mild. He received small sympathy from the other cattlemen in his district. They all knew him to be penurious, grasping — in short, a tightwad of the first water. Samson knew they knew it, but it mattered to him not the slightest. Money was his god, and he clutched his religion close to his heart, caring not the least what his neighbors thought of him.

No, the contempt of his neighbors didn't bother Tuck Samson; he went along year after year in his tightfisted manner, paying the smallest wages and working his men the hardest of any stock raiser in the county. He was probably the least-liked man in the Antelope Mountain Country, and through some twist in his perverse make-up, took a sort of enjoyment in the distinction.

It had looked for a brief week or two that winter as though Samson had showed rare judgment in putting up only three quarters the amount of hay he should have. The winter — it seemed — had broken up early, the earth had commenced to show through on the higher ridges, snow was beginning to melt and course in small streams through the gullies. There were days when the sun felt almost hot. Samson had chuckled. By jeepers! he'd save money this year.

And then — then the weather had changed! The wind veered round to the north again, bringing with it the sting of driving snow. The temperature dropped down and down. There was no doubt about it now: old King Boreas had played an April fool joke on the Beartrap outfit. For five straight days the snow fell without a letup. It wasn't a soft, gentle fall. It came in a howling blizzard that drove everything before it, the frozen flakes cutting like sharp-edged spears when they slashed against bare flesh. The thermometer dropped thirty-five degrees the first two days of the storm.

The blizzard was blinding at times, and punchers out on the range were never certain whether they were headed north, south, east or west. One of them never did learn; his body was found in a coulee weeks later, after the snow had melted.

Driven by his money mania, Tuck Samson refused to put on additional help when the storm came on. Snow that had melted the previous weeks soon turned to ice, making the search for grass more difficult than ever for the stock. Cattle dropped by the dozens; once down, they stayed down to die. Only a relatively few were roused up by punchers and brought in to feed on the fast disappearing hay.

The Beartrap punchers rose before dawn, worked steadily all day in the zero climate and arrived back, half frozen to the marrow, hours after night had fallen. They gave all they had — and Tuck Samson demanded more. He raged like a wild man at times, plowing from line camp to line camp through the deep snow, cursing because he was losing stock. The only hay to be had now couldn't be got out to the Beartrap.

On the fifth day the blizzard ceased to

howl; the weather commenced to clear. The sun again emerged from behind the dank gray clouds and shed its rays over a land blanketed in white. It was still cold, though, and the sun's heat wasn't strong enough to accomplish much good. For ten days after the storm had ceased the cowboys worked like fiends. The snow was waist-deep in spots, and the weaker cattle, once they'd dropped, lacked strength to rise again.

Gradually, however, the cowboys commenced to gain the upper hand, and Samson realized that more of his herd would be saved than he had contemplated. It was the never-dying loyalty of the cowboy that had put this across, that not understandable something that forces a cowpuncher to give the best that is in him — and more — to the man who pays his wages. That, regardless of conditions, or the employer's attitude toward his men. Not one of the crew had any genuine liking for Tuck Samson, but they had hired out to him. That settled the matter: Samson was entitled to the best they had; they'd stay with him until the fight was over.

It was one day toward the third week in April that a black figure appeared against the dazzling white of the snow-blanketed country. The rider's horse ploughed stolidly through the drifts, carrying on its back a short, stocky, broad-shouldered figure, well bundled in Mackinaw, wool mittens and angora chaps.

The wide brim of the man's sombrero was tied down over his ears with a large bandanna.

The puncher had just topped a snow-drifted ridge. He stopped and glanced down a long slope of white to a point where a steer thrashed about far below him. The steer was down, struggling frantically to arise or at least swing about to face the gray, doglike animal squatting on haunches on the packed snow a few feet away.

The gray, doglike animal suddenly rose, moved in close, then swerved quickly to one side as the steer jerked out savagely with sharp horns. The gray animal backed off again, sat patiently down to await the moment when the fast-weakening steer would become too powerless to resist death.

The rider up on the rise grunted, "Huh, wolf!" He removed his mittens and slowly reached to the rifle in his saddle boot. The rifle was at his shoulder before the lobo had become aware of the man's proximity. From rider to wolf was a fairly long shot. The puncher took careful aim, hesitated, adjusted his sights a trifle, then aimed again. His finger tightened slowly about the trigger . . . a shot echoed across the cracking white silence. Instantly the wolf was up and away. The rider swore with soft impatience, levered another cartridge into the chamber, whipped up the rifle a second time. The weapon

11

spoke with sharp finality. This time the wolf dropped, half buried in a drift of snow.

"Two cartridges — hell!" the cowboy muttered disgustedly to himself. "Caliper, you're getting worse all the time with this Winchester gun. Never could shoot with anything but a hawg-laig, anyway."

He replaced the rifle in the scabbard, then made haste to draw on his mittens again as he urged the pony into motion. A few minutes later he had dismounted a few feet away from the foundered steer.

The fallen animal gazed up at him with dumb brute eyes that were a trifle antagonistic. The cowboy moved heavily around the steer, his boots sinking through snow crust, examining it closely. Finally, "Shucks, cow, you ain't hurt none. I reckon that lobo was just playing with you before he made his killing. Might be you're some weak — or are you just plain lazy? We'll see if we can't get you up. C'mon, you do your part and I'll do mine."

Walking around to the rear of the animal, he seized its tail in both hands and pulled — twisted. For a moment there was no response, then suddenly there came a bellow of rage from the tortured steer. Still, however, no movement. The cowboy's muscular hands took a firmer grip on the tail, he increased his efforts. The maddened bellowing grew stronger.

Suddenly the steer's feet braced, its body strained. The next instant it had lumbered up. The cowboy knew what to expect. He whirled and, impeded by snow and high-heeled boots, ran awkwardly to his pony and climbed into the saddle.

Where the snow was packed down from the struggle with the wolf the steer made good time. An instant later it broke through the snow crust where the going was harder. The cowboy escaped the sharp steer horns only by inches as the horse managed to jump to one side.

"Hell of a way to treat a feller," the cowboy grumbled as his horse ploughed on. He glanced hack at the steer standing looking at him. "Stay on your feet now, cow, and you'll be all right. Warm weather is due plumb shortly, I reckon. Shame on you, trying to horn me after I saved you from that lobo and got you into a respectable, upright position again! Don't you know position in life is everything? Plumb ungrateful, I calls it!"

He paused suddenly, swearing softly. "Thunderation! Why didn't I pick up that lobo before I got the steer to his feet? I reckon if I went back now that blamed steer would take after me. Oh well, the snow was right deep where that lobo went down. No use making my pony work harder'n necessary. I reckon that bounty will hold good until I

13

come out again. If the skin's chewed-up or gone I won't get it, that's all."

He still hesitated in his mind, trying to decide whether or not to brave the steer's wrath and the deeper snow where the wolf lay for the sake of the pelt, but finally decided to go on. It was growing late.

Darkness was but an hour away and he was nearing camp when off to the right he saw another cowboy driving eight straggling cows before him. Caliper drew rein to wait. "That looks like Nogales," he speculated. "Reckon I'll rest here and wait until he comes up."

A few minutes later two cows broke from the bunch of approaching animals and ambled off in different directions. Across the snow came a salvo of profanity from the cowboy herding the animals, as he sent his horse in pursuit.

"That's Nogales all right," Caliper chuckled. "I recognize his voice talking to God thataway. Maybe I can help him."

He put in his spurs and started to the rescue. It was but a few minutes' work to head off one steer while Nogales was herding back the other animal. Then Caliper fell in behind the bunch of plodding beasts, which, unusual to relate, had continued in the same direction it had been going when left to its own resources by Nogales.

The two riders moved closer until they

were riding stirrup to stirrup. Caliper said, "I thought it was you when I saw you coming. Got any tobacco? I lost mine."

Nogales, his face blue with cold, nodded. Mittens were removed and cigarettes rolled with stiff fingers. There seemed little heat from the match flame when cupped hands were held about the cigarettes, but the tobacco quickly caught and gray smoke mingled with steamy breaths on the frosty air.

"These damn cows," Nogales said disgustedly, exhaling a deep puff of smoke, "are more trouble than they're worth. Look at 'em! I found 'em down in Snake Coulee huddled in the drifts, almost ready to drop and die. There were thirteen of 'em when I started out. They been dropping off one by one. I got plumb weary of tailin' up and finally decided to let 'em go, if they ain't got sense enough to come home with me. I been since noon getting this far. Ain't it hell?"

Caliper agreed that it *was* hell. "You might just as well have let these go, too," he stated. "The hay's nearly gone. Damn Tuck Samson for a miserly, chuckle-headed scoundrel, anyway."

"You and me are the chuckle-headed ones," Nogales growled, "for working for him." Caliper nodded gloomily. After a pause Nogales asked, "Didn't you find any beefs to bring in?"

Caliper took a last fond drag on his cigarette

and chucked it away. "Nope, everything I found was strong enough to take care of itself. The range is pretty clean by this time. . . . I did find one cow playing with a lobo."

Nogales cast a quick glance sidewise, then frowned. "Where's the pelt?"

"I forgot it until too late. The cow critter kept me sort of busy after I had tailed it up. I wasn't waiting to fool around to take any skin. Had to run for my horse and then, once I was riding, I — well, you know how it is."

"I know how *you* are," Nogales growled. "You dumb-headed rannie — chucking away good bounty money that way. Ain't you ever going to learn which side your bread is buttered on?"

"Working for Tuck Samson," Caliper grinned, "I'm even forgetting there's such a thing as butter. And bread isn't so plentiful, either, when you come right down to it. Shucks, Nogales, if I ever got the money for that pelt, you'd probably just borrow and lose it playing draw poker —" He checked himself suddenly.

There was silence for a time as the two riders plodded on. It was dark now, but the cows showed up black against the white snow. Finally Caliper spoke, "It doesn't seem so cold as it did this morning."

It was a lame effort. Nogales ignored the remark and spoke regretfully. "I haven't said much, pard, but you know danged well that I'm plumb sorry about losing your money."

"Dammit," Caliper cussed ruefully, "I didn't intend to bring up that subject — ever. It just sort of slipped out, Nogales. You know I was only ribbin' you about losing that time. What the blasted hell do I care about money?"

"I know you didn't mean it, Caliper. You've been one white cowhand. Here we were with enough *dinero* to see us through the winter without working, and then I had to lose yours and mine both, trying to out-guess that poker sharp down to Cottonwood Center. I haven't said much about it. I reckon I've been too embarrassed, letting you in for a winter of tough work —"

"I'm not kicking any —" Caliper commenced.

"I know it. That's what makes it so hard. You've pitched in and not a word out of you. I'll pay you back, though, just as soon as I can get my hands on some cash."

"Forget it," Caliper growled.

"I won't forget it. I used your money and —"

"Listen, you long drink of water" — Caliper spoke with some irritation — "you bore me stiff, bellyaching about that money. What if you did lose it? Haven't we been pards, share and share alike, for a long, long time? Haven't you split your roll with me more than once when I was so broke I didn't even have makin's? . . . We'll put it this way — supposing you'd just lost your money and hadn't lost mine with it. Do you think I'd have loafed in town all winter and let you come out here to work alone? Huh!"

Caliper's voice broke a little. This thing of showing affection was getting Caliper on dangerous ground. He changed the subject abruptly. "I guess I'm the wind-brained idiot, I am, listening to you when you talked me into coming up into this Wyoming country."

"Huh! Me?" Nogales ejaculated in amazement, forgetting their former subject. "Why, it was *you* proposed this trip. You've gone crazy if you blame me. Cripes! I never have got over kicking myself for being seduced up here by you with all your fine talk. And now you're blaming *me!* Well, may I be danged!"

Caliper grinned to himself in the darkness. "You're the crazy galoot! Have you forgotten telling me about the snowcapped mountains up here in summer and the trout streams with the little blue flowers growing along the banks?"

Nogales looked at his partner in amazement. "I told you! I told you?" he exclaimed. "Why, it was *you* said all those things. And like a damn fool I let myself be persuaded to come."

"It was you that persuaded *me*," Caliper insisted. "Don't you remember saying how you'd show me a country where there was water even in the summer — not like the old desert country where everything is dried up and parched —"

"Caliper Maxwell!" Nogales said indignantly. "It was you made all those claims. You sure got a lousy memory. What's got into you trying to blame me for coming up here?"

"It was you, Nogales."

"It wasn't."

"It was. And you told about the big trees and —"

"You're loco . . . !"

By this time the matter of the money lost in the poker game was forgotten, as a heated argument broke out as to which one was responsible for this visit to the northern country. The argument was finally broken up by one of the cows, ahead of the squabbling riders, breaking away from the bunch and heading off at a tangent. Caliper took after the recalcitrant animal and in a short time headed it back where it resumed its plodding march.

Again they rode on in silence. Finally Nogales' voice broke softly through the darkness, "Caliper —"

"What's on your mind?"

"Caliper, down along the border they're starting calf roundup about now."

"Gosh! You're right. Nogales, I'd give anything to be back there again. Me, I'd sure welcome the sight of desert country and alkali and bleached bones. Too many trees up here and mountains — they're both so damned high a feller can't see the scenery. Why, I'd even be tempted to make love to a 'Pache squaw if I could be back down there."

"Me, I'm sort of sick of this country too. . . . It doesn't seem like home nohow, what with the ropes and rigs being different. And I'd like to have me some bullhide chaps again. These angoras make me feel like I was packin' a pussycat on each laig all the time."

"Yeah, I know how you feel. . . . You know, at that, this is a sort of nice country in the warm months. Reckon the trouble is with us — we're just homesick."

"That's it. We've just got a hankering for the ol' southwest border country again."

"You've hit it. There's lots of nice fellers up here, too, exceptin' —"

"Exceptin' Tuck Samson," Nogales caught him up. "Oh, this trip hasn't been a loss to us. It's been fun lots of times. And it's an education to see new country. I sure wish we had the money to just travel around all the time."

"That'd be the life all right, pard."

Their horses carried the two cowboys around a snowcapped boulder. Through the darkness an oblong of yellow light suddenly jumped into view two hundred yards away.

"Camp at last," Caliper exclaimed. "I'm plumb glad to get in. Hope the hay shoveler's got grub pile ready."

The "hay-man" met them when they arrived. "What the tarnation," he grumbled, eyeing the cows ahead of the riders, "more hospital stuff?"

"It won't be necessary to nurse 'em real tender," Nogales replied from his saddle, "but they're too weak to stay out alone. Give 'em plenty feed. That's what they need."

"Yaah," the hay-man exploded derisively. "Plenty feed! Where's it coming from? Another week and the hay will be plumb gone. . . . Well, pile off them saddles and put your broncs up. Yore beans is hot on the stove, and the cawfee's been kept at a bubble for you."

"Coffee!" Caliper exclaimed blissfully. "I'll be ready to stick my head right in the pot just as soon as we take care of these billy-be-damned, misguided examples of bovine animal life."

"You mean them cows?" The hay-man looked blankly at Caliper. "Shucks, forget 'em and go get yore fodder. Steve's out back. He'll come runnin' when I call and help me with the dang beef critters."

2. "I Aim to Get My Pay"

Nogales Scott drained the last drop from his coffee cup, pushed back his empty plate, sighed with satisfaction and reached for his sack of Durham and cigarette papers. He was a tall, rangy individual, at present dressed in faded blue overalls, woolen shirt and riding boots. His features were rugged, as though hewn from living rock — nose slightly aquiline, firm chin and a smile that lighted up his candid gray eyes like a spring morning.

He sifted some tobacco into a cigarette paper, then tossed the sack across to Caliper. Caliper had other names, but they weren't often brought out to view. He endorsed his pay checks with a plain C. Maxwell. As a matter of fact the C stood for Cadwallader. Entirely ignorant that the name Cadwallader signified "battle arranger" — and it was very appropriate — the cowboy always felt there was something sissy about the name. Folks who asked what the C stood for were always answered with a scowl. After that they took one look at his bowed legs and decided that C was the initial letter of Caliper. Someway the name stuck to the cowboy, and people forgot, if they ever knew, that he had any other name. Nogales was one of the few who was in on the secret, his own Christian name having been derived from the fact that he was born in a town called Nogales.

Caliper was the direct antithesis of Nogales, being broad where the other was slim, short where his pardner was long. Only in temperament did the two agree. Caliper's face was bland, round, good-natured. His blond hair always looked as though he'd just crawled out of his blankets, and his drowsy blue eyes lent emphasis to that impression.

On the whole they both looked to be the average type of cowpuncher. The two had weathered so many storms together that each always knew what to expect from the other. In a fight their teamwork was something at which to marvel. At times their remarks to each other were nothing short of insults, but there was always an accompanying grin to alleviate the thrusts. They understood each other, these two. Both were mature men, but their hearts were those of boys — playboys. Under the playful front, however, ran a shrewd vein of seriousness.

They sat smoking, silently enjoying their after-supper cigarettes. The door of the cabin burst suddenly open. The hay-man came in cursing, his partner, Steve, behind him. Steve was a dour-faced man who never had a great deal to say. The door banged shut again, and Steve retired to a chair behind the stove and fell into a doze. The hay-man dropped wearily to a chair at the table. "Damn this pitchin' hay all day and all night, too," he grumbled, "when there ain't enough hay to go round."

Nogales winked at Caliper and asked, "Why don't you ask Samson why he doesn't get in more?"

The hay-man glowered at the questioner. "Do you think I'm plumb cuckoo? I asked him today to have some bacon sent out. Gawd! You should have seen him. You'd think I'd asked him for his heart —"

Caliper cut in, "It probably wouldn't have affected him any worse if you had."

The hay-man nodded. "He nigh took my head off. 'Bacon,' he says, 'bacon! Don't you lazy cowhands do nothin' but eat?' I told him a few things about how you was workin', but he wa'n't satisfied. By cripes! It won't be many weeks more before I'll be quittin' the old moss-backed so-and-so."

"What was he here today for?" Nogales asked. "Don't tell me he brought our pay?"

"Naw," the hay-man replied disgustedly. "He just come around to see was everybody working and to get 'em to work harder."

"It's payday," Caliper said. "Did he leave our pay?"

The hay-man shook his head. "I got my pay, though. Told him I wanted it plumb prompt. He tried to put me off at first —

said he didn't have it with him. I told him he could fork his own hay then, if he wouldn't pay what was due. That made him come across. Gosh, how that old skinflint hates to part with money."

"He sure does," Caliper agreed. He speculated grimly for a few moments, then, "For two cents I'd ride over to the ranch house and make him give me my pay." He rose and went to the window, stood looking out at the gleaming snow now touched with moonlight. "Yep, I sure got a notion to ride to the ranch and make him fork over. It's bad enough living at a line camp this way without being put off every time you got money due. I got a good notion to saddle up right now and have it out with that penny-squeezing miserly —"

"Yes, you have," Nogales laughed skeptically, "— not! I can see you stirring away from the stove on a night like this. Don't fret, cowboy, we'll get what's coming to us."

Caliper nodded glumly and remained at the window. "I know we'll get it in time but I'd just like the satisfaction of making Samson pay money when it's due."

The hay-man commented, "I noticed when I came in it was warmin' up some."

Caliper left the window and went to the door of the log-constructed cabin. He went out and closed the door behind him. He stood outside, sniffing the keen air. Suddenly his nostrils twitched a little. He turned and opened the door calling, "Nogales, come outside a minute."

Nogales lifted his lean, rangy frame from the chair and made his way outdoors. The door closed behind him. The two pardners stood there in the open under the stars.

Caliper waited impatiently, then, "Smell it?" he asked. "Do you get it?"

Nogales sniffed the breeze. "Kind of balmylike, isn't it?"

"Cowboy, yes! It's the old chinook a-coming. When you smell that balmy chinook breeze, spring's sure on the way. That's what the Indians used to say. Nogales, spring isn't far off."

The two returned to the cabin, sat talking a while. Caliper seemed rather absent-minded, as though his thoughts were on far-away subjects. Suddenly he arose, buckled on his belt and gun, slipped into Mackinaw and chaps.

Nogales had been watching him curiously without speaking. Now he asked, "Where you heading?"

Caliper said belligerently, "I'm heading for the ranch house. I've got wages coming and I aim to get 'em. For two cents I'd make the round of the line camps and get more of the boys to go in with me. I'd like to throw a shock into that tightwad."

"Ain't no use of you going to the ranch

house to see Samson," the hay-man said, " 'cause he won't be there. He told me he was going to stay in Cottonwood Center to-night."

"Good," Caliper said promptly. "I won't have so far to ride after all."

Nogales accused unfeelingly, "You've gone crazy in the brainpan, Caliper. One sniff of warm weather coming and it goes to your head."

"Come along with me," Caliper invited. "I aim to get my pay. If you're with me it'll save me asking for your wages along with mine."

"Who? . . . Me?" Nogales half shouted his astonishment. "Do you think I'm crazy too? Nothing doing! Any man who'll make a ride like that tonight hasn't got any more brains than a cottontail. Through all that snow, too. Think what would happen if your bronc slips and breaks a laig."

"I'm thinking." Caliper grinned. "What happens? All the answer I get is that the bronc has three laigs left."

"That's all the answer I'd expect *you* to get," Nogales sneered. "It takes brains to figure that you might get tumbled off in the snow when he went down. Maybe you get hurt bad. It's not warm weather yet by a long shot. Maybe you might take a long sleep in the snow — you and your bronc."

Caliper chuckled. "That'd be all right so

long as he didn't kick the covers off me. I'm dang sure he wouldn't talk in his sleep."

"No use trying to talk sense to you," Nogales said disgustedly. "You ain't got the intellect to understand me, anyway."

"That's not the question," Caliper retorted. "I gave up trying to understand *you* long ago. Decided it wasn't any use. The question is are you coming with me or ain't you?"

"I ain't you," Nogales snapped. "I'm plump tuckered. Had a tough day. Too tired to make that ride tonight. You better not stir out, either."

"I already told you what I'm going to do," Caliper said stubbornly. "I'm just asking you to come."

Nogales shook his head. "You'd better stay here, Caliper, where you can keep warm. Nobody but a danged fool would make that ride tonight. Not in cold weather. That chinook breeze didn't fool me any. I remember we had one something like it a few weeks ago. And look what's happened. You stay here. We'll see Samson in a few days. There isn't anything less than wild hawsses could drag me outside tonight."

All unmoved, Caliper went on with his preparations. The bandanna was tied down over his sombrero, his coat collar turned up. Saddle in one hand, he stood warming his bridle bit on the stove. Within a few minutes he drew on his mittens and started toward

28

the door. Here he paused, turned and spoke to Nogales, "It's your last chance. Have I got to ask you again? Coming?"

Nogales grinned and uncoiled his long length from the chair. "Certain I'm coming. Whatever gave you the idea I wasn't?"

It was a long, cold ride through the snow, but at last the lights of Cottonwood Center hove into view. Chilled to the bone as they were, the two cowboys were laughing and talking as they rode into the snow-covered town. Here they put spurs to their ponies and came tearing up to the door of the Cotton-wood Center Livery Stable as though they'd just been out on a short pleasure canter of two or three miles.

The stableman glanced at the clock as he opened the door to let them enter. "Fine time o' night to be coming here," he grumbled. "Don't you two never sleep?"

"Yeah, we tried it once," Nogales answered gravely. "Caliper, here, hasn't ever woke up. He caught that disease — what was it? — oh yes, he's what they call a somnambulist."

"I know *I'm* asleep," Caliper chuckled. "Nogales is in the same condition but don't know it. That's the only difference between us two."

The livery stable man was given detailed instructions regarding the care of the horses, then the two cowboys made their way along the snowy street, filling their lungs with frosty, clear air. It was growing warmer, no doubt of that; they could feel the snow pack beneath their feet.

Cottonwood Center was a fair-sized town but just now it was too late for many to be abroad on the streets. At present it had a sort of deserted atmosphere. Lights shone from windows here and there, but for the most part the houses were already dark and their occupants in bed.

Nogales and Caliper strode along side by side, the snow creaking a trifle under their boots. Suddenly Nogales seized Caliper's arm and came to a stop. "Wait," he hissed. "Who's that coming?"

On the opposite side of the street, some distance away, a bulky individual was walking with important strides along the snow-encrusted sidewalk. The man had just been passing the night light in a shopwindow when Nogales spied him.

"It's Old Sleuth, isn't it?" Nogales whispered an instant later, peering sharply up the street.

Caliper nodded, frowning. "Yeah. What about him? What did you grab me like this for? He hasn't anything on us."

"Shh! Not so loud, pard. I was just thinking what a fathead that sheriff is. Sheriff Horatio Trautz! Gosh, he's important to himself. I reckon he's making a last tour of the burg to see that nobody doesn't steal any fence gates or something. It seems like we should give him an excuse to work off some of his ambition. You know —"

Caliper was commencing to get the idea. "I was just thinking," he cut in, "about that time when we first hit this town, year ago last fall. 'Member? And how Trautz tried to pin that rustling job on us. Not that we'd had anything to do with it but we were strangers here, and Trautz felt he should make an arrest so folks would think he was on the job."

"We proved we were innocent of that."

"Sure, but we never did properly square up with Trautz."

"Just what I was thinking when I first saw him. C'mon!"

The two darted into a passageway between two buildings. Stooping, they commenced rolling snowballs with much earnestness and subdued laughter. By the time Sheriff Horatio Trautz, making his way along the opposite side of the street, had drawn abreast of their hiding place, they had quite a sizable pile of ammunition before them.

"Don't fire until you can see the whites of their eyes." Nogales chuckled, seizing a snow-ball in each fist. He raised up and peered around the corner of the building. His arm came back, then shot forward. . . .

A sudden howl of surprise sounded across

the street. The snowball had taken the bulky sheriff directly behind his left ear and knocked off his hat. He turned in angry surprise — just in time to receive a flying ball of snow from Caliper's accurate hand. It landed full in Trautz' face! It was too dark between the buildings where Caliper and Nogales were concealed for the sheriff to see who they were, but he knew the direction from which the shots were coming.

Trautz started across the street on the run. Another snowball struck him — and another. In an instant the air was filled with the flying white missiles. The two cowboys were throwing as fast as they could stoop for ammunition and let fly! Some of their shots missed the mark altogether, but the majority found a target.

Trautz grunted angrily and staggered back under the attack; his foot slipped and he went down in a deep drift on the cowboys' side of the street. Floundering once more to his feet, he struck his head on a near-by hitch rack and went down a second time. Without waiting to rise he lost his temper and pawed under his overcoat for his six-shooter. . . . There came a vivid stab of orange flame, and a bullet ripped into a plank wall far to the left.

"He's shooting at the wrong shadow," Nogales whispered, smothering a laugh.

"It was meant for us, though," declared the

belligerent Caliper. "What say we shoot it out with the so-and-so?"

"No, you fighting cock, our snowballs are all gone. C'mon!"

Seizing his companion's arm, Nogales dashed to the rear of the building which had sheltered them, then turned and ran along the backs of the buildings. From the street came more firing. Lights commenced to appear along the way. Voices demanded to know what was the trouble? Trautz, too angry to speak coherently, was shouting something that had to do with his being attacked by bandits. The street listened a moment, then, hearing nothing but Trautz, a sudden derisive laugh went up. Then angry voices at being disturbed. Someone advised the sheriff to go home and sleep off his drunk.

Laughing and stumbling through the deep snow, Caliper and Nogales finally reached the back door of the Grizzly Bear Saloon. Flinging open the door, they came bursting in, then closed it behind them and commenced stamping snow from their boots. The barroom was empty except for the presence of Bourbon John, proprietor and bartender, who was dozing fitfully on a stool behind one end of the rough board bar. In the center of the room a big, potbellied stove sent forth welcome heat from its cherry-red sides.

Bourbon John came awake as the cowboys entered. He straightened up with a startled,

"What the hell! I was just dreaming I heard shooting down the street. It must be true —"

Nogales cut in, "Quick, set us up a couple of drinks, John. We'll tell you about it later."

Bourbon John, noting their laughter, decided nothing serious had taken place. He did as requested. Nogales and Caliper were already shedding coats and chaps and hanging them on pegs in one corner of the room. Then they hastened across to the bar, still grinning. Nogales said, "We've just been settling an old score, John. Nobody was hurt — except maybe for his feelings."

Caliper, on his way to the bar, had seized from one of the card tables ranged across the room, four or five empty whisky glasses that had stood there. These he placed on the bar near the two clean glasses and bottle of Old Crow the bartender had set before the cowboys. To judge from the glasses Nogales and Caliper had been in the Grizzly Bear Saloon at least an hour.

Nogales downed his drink. "Trautz been in lately?" he asked.

"Not for the last two hours," Bourbon John replied. He grinned widely. "You two been deviling our fat-headed law officer? He needs somebody to wake him up —"

"He'll probably be in here again in a minute," Caliper said swiftly. "Maybe we should be enjoying ourselves with a song when he arrives, Nogales."

34

"Bright idea," Nogales agreed. "It'll make things look better. Let's have 'Columbo.'"

Caliper nodded without speaking, winked and took up the first strains of that famous song:

"In fourteen hundred ninety-two
Columbo sailed the ocean —"

At that moment the bulky Trautz waddled through the door and slammed it angrily behind him. He was red-faced and bedraggled, covered with snow from head to foot, panting angrily.

Bourbon John said innocently, "It must be snowing again."

Sheriff Trautz ignored the remark, though it sent his blood pressure into swift ascent. He eyed the two punchers singing, standing at the bar, apparently unaware of his presence. Some intuition told Trautz that the seat of his trouble lay here, and yet he couldn't feel certain of it. All he saw was two very drunken cow punchers striving to harmonize in an off key. Judging by the number of empty glasses at their elbows, they'd been making a good job of their celebrating.

"What's the idea of all this noise?" Trautz demanded angrily. "This is a fine time of night to be —"

"He thought the world was round-o-o-o!"

Nogales interrupted, his deep bass booming discordantly through Caliper's squeaky tenor. The singing continued while the sheriff strove to make himself understood. Somehow he couldn't even gain the attention of the two cowboys. Trautz commenced to even doubt that they had seen him enter the Grizzly Bear, though that thought punctured his vanity no little.

"What's the matter, Sheriff?" Bourbon John asked gravely. "You look some messed up."

"Gang ambushed me," Trautz puffed, "— seven or eight of 'em — maybe more. Jumped me when my back was turned — had me down in the snow — they were hitting me on the head, with their gun bar'ls — trying to subdue me. I fit 'em off — nearly captured two of 'em — just 'bout ready to slip the handcuffs on 'em when the rest of the gang — came to the rescue — they escaped. They pulled triggers on me then — bullets was flying like hail around me. I throwed off one man, then another. Then — I got my own gun — in action — and they run —" Trautz broke off suddenly to ask, "How long them — two Beartrap cow-willies — been in — here?" He cringed as Nogales struck a particularly sour note.

Bourbon John raised his voice above the sound of the singing. "What did you say?"

"In the middle of the ocean,

36

Columbo he got blotto —"

"I said," yelled Trautz, barely able to make himself heard above the maudlin voices of the two range troubadours, "how long have them two been in here? No, I didn't say anything 'bout beer. How — long — them — two — been — in — *here?* Can you hear that?"

"Oh — I should say" — Bourbon John cocked a grave eye at the old clock on one end wall — "I should say they been here 'bout an hour and a half. Why?" he asked loudly.

"Can't be them two then," Trautz grumbled, half to himself. He looked disappointed. "I thought mebbe they was two of the gang that jumped me."

"What did you say?" Bourbon John half shouted.

". . . *that sunuvagun, Columbo-o-o-o!*" bawled the two cowboy voices, bringing the song to a long-drawn out, temporary conclusion.

Trautz glared angrily at the pair. "John," he threatened darkly, "you'd better clean up your place. You got too many vicious characters hanging around here, and —"

"For forty days and forty nights-s-s-s,
They sailed the ocean blue-ooo-oo-o-o —"

Again the singers interrupted the sheriff.

37

Trautz swore vigorously, turned and stamped heavily and in deep disgust out of the saloon.

The instant the door closed behind him Nogales and Caliper quieted down. Bourbon John eyed them severely for a few moments. "Can't say I blame Trautz for leaving," he said unfeelingly, though his eyes twinkled, "them singing voices of yours sounds like somebody tearing up rags. If I ain't bad mistook you've plumb spoiled Trautz' ear for music!"

3. Another Score Settled

When the howls of laughter had died down, Bourbon John continued, "And it ain't only your voices I object to. That was a nice song, now, wa'n't it? I'm plumb ashamed of both of you singing that way right in front of the upholder of the morals of our little community." He grinned suddenly. "That beef-bodied old fossil will get something on you two yet. He's been aching to throw you both in the jug ever since that time you made a monkey of him, when he couldn't tie that rustling job on you."

Nogales and Caliper straightened their faces with an effort. Gone was all trace of their hastily acquired intoxication.

"Did you hear him?" laughed Nogales. "Said a gang jumped him — and it was only us throwing snowballs!"

"Yeah" — Caliper went off into another fit of laughter, choking on the words — "seven or eight of 'em — but he fought 'em off. Whew! What a windbag Trautz is!"

Nogales wiped the tears from his eyes and slowly sobered. "Thanks, Bourbon, for backing our play. We'll do as much for you some time if you ever need us to defy that upright arm of the law."

"Snowballed him, eh?" Bourbon John said disgustedly. "Hell's bells! I thought maybe you'd half killed him from the way he talked when he came in. Whatever he got the old puddin'head deserved."

They had another drink. "Have you seen Tuck Samson?" Caliper asked, suddenly remembering the original reason for the trip to town.

"Yes, he was in —" Bourbon John paused. "That reminds me, the postmaster left a letter here for Samson to take out to Nogales. I reckon Samson forgot to take it. Here —" Bourbon John reached to his back bar and handed a sealed letter to Nogales.

Nogales took the letter, studied the return address in one corner: *"Tomkins & Smithers, Attorneys at Law, Chicago, Illinois,"* he read slowly, frowning. "Now what in the devil have I done to get tangled up with the law?"

Caliper observed pessimistically, "Betcha it's a breach-of-promise suit."

"Can't be," Nogales responded promptly. "I learned that gal had a husband." He looked at the letter, turning it over and over. "This has sure chased me around a lot of places. I wonder what it's about."

Caliper suggested dryly, "Why don't you open it? There might be a hint inside."

Nogales accepted the suggestion, opened the letter and read it. He commenced again at the top and re-read the words on the sheet

40

of paper. A strange look appeared on his face as he perused the closely typed message. His jaw dropped in sudden amazement. Open-mouthed, he stared with unbelieving eyes at Caliper and Bourbon John, then back to the letter again.

Caliper and Bourbon John stared back, awaiting an explanation. Nogales tried to speak, stammered, his lips moved futilely without sound. Words simply wouldn't come.

"Nogales," Caliper commenced sarcastically at last, "you should be congratulated on the fluent flow of your eloquence. You're just full of information, you are. What is it, a bill for a new saddle you never paid for, a list of prospects from a matrimonial agency or a correspondence course in working over cattle brands?"

"It's — it's —" Nogales commenced when he was interrupted by the opening of the saloon door. Nogales looked up, caught sight of the long scrawny figure of Tuck Samson entering the saloon and hastily stuffed the letter into his pocket.

A joyful light had entered Nogales' gray eyes at sight of Tuck Samson. Nogales had stood just about as much of Samson's tyranny as it was possible for one man to contend with. More than once he had been on the point of quitting, but the thought of the money owing to Caliper had constrained him. But now, Nogales considered, it was time to

41

speak without restraint.

"So you two are here, are you?" Samson croaked disagreeably. "Sheriff Trautz jest came inter the hotel and told me a couple of my punchers was getting drunk in the Grizzly Bear. I —"

Nogales snapped, "Samson, you might just as well have stayed away. Nobody wants to buy you a drink."

"How's that?" Samson was a trifle deaf. He cupped one hand about his right ear and waited for Nogales to repeat the words.

Caliper was alarmed at Nogales' blunt speech. He liked Samson no better than did his pardner, but, after all, it was still cold weather and a job was a job. Samson might take offense and fire Nogales. If Nogales left, so would Caliper.

Nogales was repeating, "Samson, I said you might as well stay away. Nobody wants to buy you a drink."

Caliper cut in loudly, glibly. "Nogales says," Caliper almost shouted, "that you should have stayed in the hay. It's too noisy here to think."

Samson nodded understandingly, "Yeah, Sheriff Trautz said you was making a lot of noise. Told me you was both drunk. I reckon you ain't drunk, yet — but you got no business being in town. What's the idee of coming to Cottonwood Center when I'm payin' you good money to remain at camp?"

"What good money?" Nogales sneered.

Caliper flared up suddenly, "Paying us good money, are you? I note you didn't leave our pay at camp today. We come in for it. That's what brought us to town."

"Oh, it is, is it?" Samson growled disagreeably. "Well, I'll show you you can't take the bit in yore mouths thataway. I'll teach you a lesson, I will. Here you should be at camp and you come to town without my permission. Just for that I figure I'll fine you both one day's wages —"

"You'll do nothing of the sort," Nogales cut in with deadly calmness. "We don't bluff easy. As to coming to Cottonwood Center tonight — that's our business! We've worked hard and done our best to save your stock — in spite of the fact you've done *your* best to prevent that."

Caliper looked at Nogales in astonishment. Nogales didn't often fly off the handle in such fashion. Something new was in the air.

Samson snarled at Nogales, "What do you mean — I did *my* best to prevent it?"

Nogales warmed to his subject: "Exactly what I said. If you'd had the brains of a louse you'd have put up more hay. But no! You're too afraid to spend a few extra dollars to do anything like that. You're so low down you don't even furnish the cook enough grub to spread a decent meal. I wouldn't be surprised if you counted the grains of sugar every time you come in the kitchen. And wasn't it you that made your horse wear green glasses so you could feed him sawdust, and he'd think it was grass? And not only that, but —"

"You're fired!" Samson shouted hotly. "I'll have no man on my pay roll talk to me that way. You're fired!"

"We're not fired," Nogales snapped back. "We've quit. Caliper and I decided to quit on our way into town. We made up our minds that we wouldn't work for you any longer."

"You can't quit!" Samson shouted, enraged. "I'll hold up your wages —"

"And that's something else we decided," Nogales said calmly. "We knew you'd try something crooked so we decided we'd square matters in a way you didn't like if you turned ornery on us."

Caliper's eyes widened. This was the first he'd heard of any such arrangement but he flew loyally to his pardner's assistance in the verbal barrage. "Yep, that's what," Caliper stated. "I told Nogales I wasn't going to work for an old skinflint like you any longer. I said to Nogales, I said, 'Nogales, we'll quit the old moss-backed, wind-broken sunuva-sheepherder!' "

Nogales grinned through his heat. "That's what, Samson. It's not as if we were quitting you in the dead of winter. We've done all we could, and like's not you've just been waiting for an excuse to hang the sack on us, seeing spring isn't far off. It'd be just like you, you buckle-necked, penny-pinching buzzard. You're so tight you squeak like a new saddle. I hope I'm hung if I ever again draw down pay from such a worthless, mean, windjammin', beetle-backed skunk as you. If I had my way I'd make you eat the muddy hay you've been feeding your critters, you sway-backed, gall-sored, flannel-mouthed, spavined —"

And so it went for five minutes. Caliper always swore it lasted a half-hour but then Caliper always was prone to exaggeration. Nogales' wrath had been piling up all winter and now he let off steam in deadly earnest. Bourbon John and Caliper listened with an ever-growing admiration for Nogales' inexhaustible fund of insulting epithets. The best that can be said for Samson was that he deserved every word of the tirade. For the sake of saving a few dollars he had daily, all winter long, risked the lives of both men and stock.

Samson's face was growing redder and redder; the veins stood out on his forehead as Nogales talked. Eventually he found his tongue. "I'm not taking that from any man!" he yelled apoplectically, one hand throwing back his coat as he reached for his holster. "Go for your iron!"

Before he could draw Samson found himself staring into the long blue barrel of

Nogales' steadily held six-shooter.

"Take your hand off your lead slinger right now," Nogales said grimly, "and produce your checkbook instead. Caliper and I are aiming to draw what's due us. C'mon, get busy!"

Samson suddenly subsided as he looked into the round black hole at the end of Nogales' .45. "I ain't got a checkbook with me," he growled, "nor any money, either. You'll have to wait for your money."

"I think you're a liar," Nogales said calmly, "and we're not waiting, either." He turned to Bourbon John, asking, "How you fixed for cash, John?"

Bourbon John admitted he had a few hundred dollars in the iron safe he kept under his bar. "Just in case you're figuring on me taking Tuck's note for the amount due you," he offered, "I'll be glad to do it. I can turn the note over to the bank first thing in the morning and be sure of getting my money."

Samson darted a look of hate at Bourbon then growled, "All right, all right, I'll pay. I ain't signin' no notes to anybody." He drew a roll of bills from his pants' pocket and reluctantly commenced to peel off the requisite amount.

Nogales warned, "None of your short-changing ideas, either, Samson, or I aim to bend my six-gun across your head."

Samson colored, then went pale. He finished counting out the money and handed the bills to Caliper and Nogales. "And don't come whining to me, begging a job when that's gone," he snarled. "I know cowhands and I know you two tramps won't have money very long. But don't ask me —"

"I'm only asking you one thing," Nogales cut in. "I'm asking you to get out of here before I have to throw you out. And don't ever come into any place where I'm drinking again. Now get out!"

Samson commenced to back toward the door, fright written plainly on his features. Caliper suggested hopefully, "Let's wash his face in the snow outside."

At the words Samson turned and ran hastily from the Grizzly Bear, the door slamming on his heels.

"Shall we take after him and tumble him in the snow?" Caliper grinned.

"By cripes!" Bourbon John laughed. "You fellers told Samson what's what. He's needed that sort of handling for a long time. Maybe it will teach him a lesson."

Nogales answered Caliper, "Why waste any more time on him? We got more important things to do."

Caliper suddenly sobered and turned to Nogales. "Well, that's that," he said in a subdued tone. "We told him what we thought and we got our pay — but where are we? We've got two months' pay between us. What do we use for money when that's gone? Nobody will be hiring for quite a spell yet."

Nogales' eyes twinkled, but he looked grave. "Caliper," he accused, "you certainly got us into a fine jam losing your temper thataway. You should have looked ahead a mite —"

"Losing *my* temper!" Caliper said indignantly. "It was *you* that laid Samson out. You started the whole thing —"

Nogales shook his head regretfully. "That terrible temper of yours certainly has made us a lot of trouble. You should have known better than to get Samson all riled up that way. Did you think you could get away with a thing like that without being fired? You sure got a crazy streak in you some place. You might have had a little consideration for me and not pulled me into your argument." He pretended irritation. "I don't see what got into you! Now there's nothing for me to do but take your money and put it with mine and win us enough to live on until we get a good job."

The corners of Caliper's mouth twitched. "As a poker player, Nogales," he drawled, "you're one hell of a good cowpuncher. Howsomever, here's my money. Take it with my blessing. We might as well be broke as half primed!"

Nogales howled with delight and seized Caliper by the shoulders, whirled him around half a dozen times and ended up at the bar. "Caliper, old sox," he grinned, "we don't have to worry about getting a job ever again. We don't work any more. We're rich, cowboy, rich! Understand? Let's drink on it."

Caliper gazed in amazement at his pardner then turned to Bourbon John. "I guess maybe we'd better get him to a doctor, John," he said sadly. "Getting money out of Samson seems to have affected his mind. I never knew poor old Nogales was subject to brain storms, but maybe the hard winter's work has wore him plumb down to insanity."

"Insanity, nothing," Nogales beamed. "I'm telling you straight. It's all in that letter I got from those law sharps in Chicago. It seems I'm the only living relative of Angus MacLaren, the man who —"

"Angus MacLaren, the Chicago meat packer?" Bourbon John asked in amazement.

"The same," Nogales nodded. "I knew he was mixed into my family some way but I never gave it a thought. Anyway, MacLaren died suddenly without ever having made a will. He didn't have any family — never married. This letter says I get the whole estate — packing interests and everything — all his businesses." He paused suddenly. "I suppose I should be grieving some but never having known my deceased relative, it's going to be sort of difficult to go into mourning. Besides, MacLaren died nearly a year ago. The lawyers have been all this time trying to trace me. What do you think of it, pard?"

Caliper smiled and warmly shook hands. "Gosh, Nogales, that's good news. You always had some good luck coming. You can do some real loafing now."

"*I* can do some loafing? *We* can do some loafing! Get this straight, Caliper, what's mine is yours. We're sharing like we've always done —"

Caliper shook his head. "Nope! Not me. We've come to the parting of the ways, Nogales. I never was cut out to attend any afternoon tea in society or wear a monkey suit with tails down behind —"

"You dang bullheaded rannie!" Nogales exploded. "Do you think I intend to wear boiled shirts and go in for that stuff? Get squared around and listen to me. We've been wishing we had enough money to get back to the border. Here's our opportunity. Can't you understand? There's enough money for both of us. We're millionaires!"

Caliper refused to be moved. "Look here, Nogales," he said seriously, "I appreciate what you want to do and all that but I'm not sponging on any man's money. Me, I'll work for a living before I'll loaf on a friend."

Nogales suddenly appeared to give in. "All right, you simple-minded pack animal, I'll work with you. But first we're going to Chicago where I can put my estate — guess that sounds spooky, eh? — on its proper basis, as the lawyers request. I got to go there and sign my name to some papers or something. After we've looked the town over, we'll head back home and start punchin' cows again —"

He stopped suddenly and commenced to put on his coat and sombrero.

"Where you going?" Caliper asked.

"I'm heading down to the hotel to look at a timetable. There's a train comes through Cottonwood Center sometime tomorrow morning, but I don't know the exact time. I don't want that we should miss getting to Chicago and back as soon as possible."

"May I be strung up for a hawss thief," Caliper stated with no little firmness, "if I'll go to Chicago and have a good time on your money!"

Nogales continued his preparations for departure without speaking. When he had finished and drawn on his mittens he took down Caliper's coat from its peg and brought it to his friend. "Put 'er on," he said.

Caliper slammed his hat down on the floor. "I said I wasn't going," he declared emphatically, "and I meant what I said!"

Nogales tossed the coat impatiently on the bar and started away. At the door he paused and turned, spoke earnestly, "Caliper, if you're going to be so danged obstinate about a few lousy dollars it's li'ble to break up our friendship. . . . Either you come with me, or

I'll give every danged cent of that money I inherited to some charity institution — say, the Home for Retired Sheepherders!"

Caliper's mouth dropped open. He looked into his pardner's eyes and saw he meant every word he had spoken. . . . Retired sheepherders? . . . *Sheepherders!* The idea was unthinkable to a bred-in-the-bone cowman.

Nogales flung open the door, then whirled back. "You coming with me or aren't you?"

Caliper grinned and picked up his coat. "Certain I'm coming! Whatever gave you the idea I wasn't?"

4. Action in Orejano

Of their trip to Chicago the least said the better. The two didn't drink — too much. Nor were they arrested — except once when the pure exuberance of animal spirits led Nogales into giving a demonstration of roping, with a mounted policeman on the other end of the rope. Naturally, this did break up a parade for the time being. However, the presiding judge at the hearing, deciding that all cowpunchers were a trifle insane, anyhow, let them off with a light fine.

Anyway, nothing serious happened during the two weeks' stay in Chicago, and by the end of May, Nogales' business affairs being concluded, the two pulled out of the Windy City, glad once more to be heading west. Once away from city pavements they commenced the long ride — in the saddle — toward the Mexican border.

For the most part Caliper and Nogales just loafed that summer. Caliper had made a killing at the gaming table shortly after their trip commenced and, being well heeled, had not complained at the slow method of travel.

It was getting along toward the end of August when, topping a rise of ground, they saw, sprawled in a rocky hollow far below them, the little town of Orejano. By that time the grass had turned from green to dusty brown, and the sage was looking just a little more twisted and dried.

The two cowboys reined their mounts in to view the scene. "Now that's what I call God's country," Nogales exclaimed. "I've never been down in this neck of the range before but I'm betting that little town we see is full of hell. It's too far from organized law enforcement to be anything else. It looks familiar — just as all these 'dobe settlements do that I've been hankering to see. I don't reckon we're more than fifty miles from the border. Caliper, look at those mountains beyond the town liftin' straight up until their peaks almost touch the clouds. . . ."

"Only there aren't any clouds in that sky," Caliper put in. "It sort of gives me a feeling like we're all under a big blue glass bowl: horses, men, mountains, sage and everything."

Nogales nodded blissfully. "This air smells good, too. It seems to be siftin' right down between those mountain peaks. And the mountains just about got the place hemmed in. I'll bet there isn't much travel through here. And there's good grazing land — then comes rocks and some chaparral —"

"Then the mountains and beyond them — alkali desert," Caliper put in with enthusiasm.

"We can't see it from here, but I know it's there. You can't get away from it, Nogales, there's no country in the world like the ol' Southwest."

"You peeped a mouthful, cowboy," Nogales agreed.

They started on, the horses picking their way carefully down the long slope. Clumps of mesquite, manzanita and catclaw were passed. Prickly pear grew in abundance, huge masses of it towering above the heads of the riders as they passed. Blue quail whirred up from the brush. High, upstanding slabs of outcropping rock commenced to appear. In places the trail made rough going, and the ponies made but little headway. Several varieties of cactus and sage marked the way.

After all it is a question whether Orejano with its winding dusty street could be termed a town. Call it a settlement and let it go at that. For the most part the buildings were of adobe structure, the homes of the Mexicans being ranged along the southern side of the street. Across from these were the Americanos and the stores and shops. One building with a high, wooden, false front displayed a sign proclaiming it to be the general store, which meant that almost anything could be purchased there, from cartridges to chili peppers all the way down the line to puncher equipment and picks and shovels.

Next to the general store stood the Apache

Saloon, owned by an Americano but presided over by a half-breed, one Mike Artora, who served drinks with dispatch but little neatness. There were a few other miscellaneous places of commercial enterprise: restaurants, a barber shop, a couple of more saloons and so on. There was little order in the layout of the town. All buildings were scattered about helter-skelter, as though some gigantic hand had been using them as dominoes and, growing weary of the game, had impatiently settled the matter by dropping them in an untidy scattering. For the rest Orejano was a hodgepodge of hitch racks, mangy dogs, wet-nosed children and sleepy, barefooted Mexicans.

The only thing that kept Orejano alive was the patronage of the cattlemen from surrounding ranches. True, a pair of railroad tracks cut across one corner of the settlement, where a group of shipping pens had been constructed, but, except in the fall months when cattle were being shipped, the train made few stops at the tiny 'dobe station.

It was nearing three in the afternoon when the two pardners rode into Orejano. Drowsy-eyed Mexicans slumbered in the shadows between buildings or awoke reluctantly to eye dully the two cowboys riding down the middle of the street. A few cowmen were seen on the street, walking along beneath the wooden awnings extending from buildings to shield passersby from the broiling heat of the southwest sun. One or two glanced curiously at Nogales and Caliper and continued on their way.

Nogales and his companion were only a short distance from the Apache Saloon when a shot was heard. The next instant the swinging doors of the place banged apart, and a lean-jawed young cowpuncher backed out, spurts of flame and smoke darting from the six-shooter in his right hand!

Shooting as he retreated to the middle of the street, the man swiftly turned and ran to the shelter of a pile of beer cases before a saloon on the opposite side of the road. Dropping flat behind this barricade, he held his fire and waited.

The next instant three tough-looking half-breeds burst through the swinging doors, guns in their hands. They looked quickly along the length of the road. The man behind the beer cases sent a shot winging towards them and it ripped splinters from one of the swinging doors. This directed the breeds' gaze to the cowman across the street. A burst of fire left their hands to thud into beer cases, then they turned and scurried back to the interior of the Apache.

Before they could enter the saloon, two hard-bitten cowpunchers appeared to bar the way. Jerking his gun, one of them spoke in threatening tones to the breeds, driving them back to the edge of the saloon porch. Reluctantly, the three breeds commenced to throw lead in the general direction of the beer cases. Gunfire answered gunfire, but no direct hits were scored.

The other man behind the breeds was just drawing his gun when he glanced along the street and saw Caliper and Nogales approaching on their ponies. He eyed them belligerently, his gun muzzle tilted a trifle in their direction as though warning them to take no part in this fight.

Again the cowman behind the barricade fired. One of the breeds spun half around . . . dropped to the porch. Struggling to his feet, he staggered inside the Apache, followed by curses from the two cowpunchers.

Nogales and Caliper had reined to a stop to see what was happening. "Huh!" Nogales spoke suddenly. "There's still four to one left. I don't like those odds, Caliper. What say we equalize matters?"

Caliper's gun was already out. He sent a bullet whining towards the feet of the two punchers on the saloon porch. "Going to sit there all day just talking about it?" Caliper laughed.

His fire was returned, kicking up dust at his pony's feet. Caliper fired again, but the object of his aim had already fled to the interior of the saloon.

Nogales had fired as he spoke. The puncher who had first urged on the breeds whirled sidewise and fell against the building, his gun dropping from a broken arm. This was too much to take. The two remaining breeds went panicky and crowded back through the swinging doors. The puncher swayed, then staggered in at their heels.

Nogales and Caliper spurred forward. They dropped from their ponies just as the man behind the beer cases rose to his feet. For a moment he didn't say anything — just stood looking in surprised appreciation at these two cowmen in denim overalls and sombreros who had come to his rescue. Their wide batwing *chaparejos* hung from their saddles. Both toted bedrolls; no doubt of it, these two were traveling and weren't on the pay roll of any local outfit.

All this the man behind the beer cases took in in a single glance, then he said, "Much obliged, fellers. You cut in at the right time but now you'd better keep moving. You've already made enemies, and this isn't a healthful town to have enemies in."

Caliper chuckled. "A man is known by the enemies he reaps."

"That part's not bothering us." Nogales smiled. "We just couldn't resist cutting in on your little shindig."

"We knew something was wrong," Caliper said, "when we saw those two hombres urging on those breeds to finish off a lone cowpoke. . . ."

He paused suddenly as a quick drumming of hoofs sounded from behind the Apache Saloon.

"Aces to tens," the man at the beer cases said, "that's Hedge Furlow making a getaway. Things must have got too hot for him. Maybe he's expecting us to follow up —"

Caliper cut in, "I've been thinking of the same thing myself. Who's Hedge Furlow?"

"He was one of the two on the porch driving them breeds to rub me out. Not the one that one of you fellers shot — that was Stan Cox —"

"Cripes! What's in a name, anyway?" Nogales interposed. "A thug by any other name would smell as bad. I'm all for clearing the atmosphere. I figure there's two breeds left and — well, does it make any difference how many more are left in that saloon?" He paused to let the idea sink in.

Caliper looked at Nogales. Nogales looked at their newfound companion in battle. He nodded. "Might as well finish it," he said tersely.

As one man the three stepped into the road, Nogales and Caliper pausing only long enough to flip their ponies' reins over the nearest hitch rack. Empty cylinders were replenished, and the three started across the street.

As they neared the Apache Saloon each man increased his pace. Each was striving to be first through the door. Nogales, having the longest legs, won a close finish.

It was dark inside the Apache after the bright sunlight of out-of-doors. For a moment Nogales couldn't see a thing. Then a sharp jet of crimson flame stabbed the gloom — a bullet cut through the bandanna at the side of Nogales' neck. His gun spoke as he passed through the swinging doors. A body crashed across a pine table in the barroom.

Nogales could see more clearly now. Two shadowy figures on his left cut loose — missed. Caliper and the other puncher were crowding close in behind Nogales, hot lead rolling from their six-shooter barrels. A gun spoke from behind the bar. Caliper whirled and threw three quick shots crashing through the flimsy board front.

The other occupants of the place took a hand — men who hadn't taken part in the battle on the street — in either throwing lead or crowding frantically through the rear door of the Apache. It became a sort of free-for-all, with the attack centering on Nogales, Caliper and their new-found friend. The fight wasn't confined to guns. Bottles were seized and thrown. Missiles went hurtling through the air. There were yells of pain and a sudden clash of splintered glass as a shelf gave way, dropping bottles and a long mirror to the floor.

The fight was over almost as quickly as it had started. It had been too dark within the Apache for accurate shooting, or the casualties would have been much greater. Four tough-looking breeds came staggering through the powder smoke, hands held high in air and yelling for mercy.

"Cease firing, men!" Caliper yelled. "The enemy has surrendered."

5. Blued-Ring Evidence

It required a few minutes to check up. Most of the customers in the place were rather bewildered over the whole business. While a rather tough-looking group they had had no part in the fight on the street. However, when Nogales and his friends had come bursting in, those who couldn't escape by the rear door had become frantic and jumped in, feeling they were acting in self-defense. Two tough-looking punchers lay dead; three Mexicans had been wounded. There were any number of black eyes and bruised heads. One man, Stan Cox, lay groaning on the floor. He had been the first to fire when the three punchers fought their way into the saloon. Nogales had already smashed Cox's arm with a shot on the porch; his first shot on entering the saloon had broken Cox's other arm.

Nogales pulled the man to his feet, while Caliper was confronting the three breeds who had started the shooting. One of them was wounded in the leg. The other two had flesh wounds that were not serious though they were at present as pale as death.

"Go on — get out!" Caliper ordered. "We're clearing out this dive. And don't come back while we're here."

There was a hasty rush toward both back and front doors. In a few moments the place was practically empty. Caliper glanced out toward the street where a crowd had gathered. "Beat it, hombres," Caliper snapped. "We're all through passing out samples." He turned back into the room.

Nogales was talking to the man with the two broken arms, Stan Cox. "Clear out, hombre," Nogales said sternly. "You're able to walk, even if your arms are plugged."

Cox staggered toward the rear door, muttering threats and within a few minutes had passed from sight. Now only Nogales, Caliper and their new-found friend were left in the saloon so far as could be seen. The saloon was a wreck, looking as though a cyclone had passed through it. Broken glasses and bottles were scattered about the floor. Flying chairs, intended for the cowboys' heads, had broken to splinters against the hard walls. Tables were overturned; table legs were broken. The long mirror that had stood behind the bar lay in a dozen broken pieces.

"Caliper," Nogales said grinning, "your terrible temper has got us into a fight again." He turned to their new friend. "Lucky none of us got hit. I wouldn't be surprised if those hombres who were in here caused as much damage to their friends as we did. It was too dark to see decent. Hope we didn't hurt any innocent bystanders."

"Not in this place you wouldn't," the other man grinned. "It's got a bad name. Anybody that was hurt deserved what he got. It was one sweet shindig all right." He paused suddenly. "I'm Lee Tanner."

Nogales took the outstretched hand. "Glad to know you, Tanner. I'm Nogales Scott. This shrinking violet with me is known as Caliper Maxwell. He's not as dumb as he looks — he couldn't be. Fact is he's not a bad hombre when you get to know him, but he sure does get me into some awful scraps."

Caliper, grinning, shook hands, then, "I wish somebody would mention a drink. I'm plumb dry. We should have checked up before we drove out those hombres and saved us a barkeep."

Something stirred behind the bar, and a round, greasy face lifted above the counter beneath which he'd been hiding. Fear still shone in the man's beady, black eyes.

Lee Tanner grinned. "Well, here's our barkeep now. Mike, you can open for business again. The celebration is over." He turned to Nogales and Caliper. "This is Mike Artora who tends bar for the proprietor of the Apache. Trot out your best, Mike — if there's anything left unbroken."

Artora fumbled about on the floor behind the bar and finally found a bottle, still intact, and three glasses. Drinks were served.

Nogales raised his glass. "Here's how!" he said, then, "Did I say *how?* I meant *now!* You know how."

Here Mike Artora broke in. "Who pays for the damage to theese so-fine barroom? My wheesky glasses? The lookeeng glass? *Socorro!* The boss he raise planty hell when he hear what 'ave happen weeth so moch of the shoot-up —"

"That's tough," Nogales said unfeelingly. "You've got our sympathy — not! You should be more careful of the customers you let come in here, Artora. Here I was coming in for a friendly drink, and some hombre throws down on us. You can't blame us for protecting ourselves, now can you? You just explain that to your boss, whoever he is. It wasn't our fault. If he insists on somebody paying for the damage, tell him to look me up. I'll try and give him what he's looking for."

"*Sí . . . sí, señor.*" Artora started to smile. "You are to pay for the dameege — no?"

"*No!*" Caliper roared. "We do not pay. Get that straight!"

Artora glowered threateningly at them. "I'm bet the Señor Krouch weel feex you for theese dameege. When he learn who —"

"Shut up, Artora," Lee Tanner said. He spun a silver dollar on the bar. "There's the price of our drinks, though I think they should be on the house." He turned to Nogales and Caliper. "If you want another

66

drink, we'll go across the street to the Blue-bonnet Bar. It's a heap better place."

Artora was still muttering threats when the three walked out.

It appeared on the street that neither Nogales nor Caliper wanted more to drink. Lee Tanner said, "I've had enough too. I hardly ever go in the Apache. Mean gang hanging out there all the time."

"Do they work for this Krouch that Artora mentioned?" Caliper asked.

Tanner said, "Well, they're not on his regular pay roll, a good many of them, but they know dang well any time they do a job that will advance Krouch's interests Krouch will pay well for it. Like I said, they're a pretty mean bunch but only when they're in a bunch. Mostly border scum, half-breeds of both Mex and Indian blood — Lord only knows how many other foreign bloods are mixed into 'em — down-at-the-heel punchers, tinhorn gamblers — you know the type. None of 'em will work regular but they're always ready to turn a dishonest penny."

"I'm glad to hear the sort of hombres they are," Nogales said, looking relieved. "I was afraid we might have hurt some innocent by-standers in that brawl."

Tanner laughed. "We might have hurt by-standers, but you can take my word for it, Nogales, that none of 'em were innocent. If you hadn't hurt them, they'd have hurt you.

Things are pretty bad in this section."

"Don't you have a sheriff or deputy here?" Caliper said.

"Not regularly," Tanner replied. "Unless something unusually bad is afoot, the sheriff stays at the county seat most of the time. There's been some talk of establishing a deputy here, but Straub Krouch has a political pull some place in the county and has managed to convince the authorities we don't need a deputy, and that appointing one to Orejano would just put an additional burden on the taxpayers."

Nogales said, "It sounds like a sweet setup for crooks. But I don't understand all of it, Tanner. You mentioned a fellow named Krouch. What's his position here? And then there was that Stan Cox who took my lead in his wings. And you called one feller — the one who ran away — Hedge Furlow. And what started all this trouble, anyway?"

Lee Tanner smiled. "I can see I'm in for telling a story, so we might as well make ourselves comfortable. Come on across the street where we can sit on the Bluebonnet Bar porch. There's some chairs there."

Nogales and Caliper followed Tanner across the roadway to a small frame building with a sign above the doorway proclaiming it to be the Bluebonnet Bar. There were some stiff-backed wooden chairs on the porch, which was shielded by a wooden awning from the hot afternoon rays of the sun. The Bluebonnet Bar was located just behind the pile of beer cases behind which Tanner had taken refuge a short time before.

As they seated themselves on the saloon porch a slim, blond fellow appeared in the bar doorway. Tanner smiled, "Hello, Johnnie. We're just resting our feet a mite. . . . Boys, this is Johnnie Armstrong, owner and proprietor of the Bluebonnet. Best bar in town."

Johnnie Armstrong shook hands and asked dryly, "Didn't I see you entering my competitor's place across the street a short spell ago?"

Nogales chuckled. "I reckon you did, Johnnie, but they didn't appear to want our business. We were no sooner inside than they tried to get rid of us. 'S'fact!"

Lee Tanner's angular, pleasant features relaxed in a broad grin. "We didn't come over here for a drink, Johnnie, but I've a hunch if you've any cold beer —"

"Cold beer!" Caliper exclaimed. "Where would he get ice down here?"

Johnnie had already nodded and withdrawn. Tanner explained, "Johnnie usually keeps a few cases of beer cold for his friends. No, he doesn't use ice. He has a wet-burlap curtain arrangement before the closet in which he keeps the beer. I never did understand the process myself, but it has something to do with evaporation keeping the beer cold. You'll see."

And see they did when Johnnie arrived with the beer. He handed each a bottle and discreetly withdrew. A few pedestrians passed and glanced curiously at the three cowmen on the porch. For a time no one spoke. Caliper and Nogales were enjoying their beer. Nogales finally asked, "How did all the fuss start, anyway, Lee?"

Tanner laughed softly. "I was playing the little game called 'Find the Rustler,' and I won. Said rustler resented my victory and — well, I reckon I'll commence farther back. I'm running the Maple-Leaf brand, out about eight miles from here. I've been losing cattle now and then but could never locate the source that was running them off —"

"That's usually the way." Nogales nodded and took a swallow of beer.

Tanner nodded and went on, "I came in here today to get a drink and my mail. I happened to see Stan Cox talking to a couple of half-breeds on the Apache porch and I heard my name mentioned. They hadn't noticed me ride in, I reckon. Cox has always had a bad reputation hereabouts, but I'm as fast as he is with a gun, and he knows it. I sort of had a hunch he had a hand in rustling my stock but I couldn't prove it of course. I heard him say something about my Maple-Leaf brand and I started across the street."

"Walked right into trouble, eh?" Caliper said.

"I wasn't thinking about that part at the

time," Tanner replied. "Just then Cox looked up and saw me coming. He made a quick grab at something in one of the breed's hands and tried to stuff it out of sight in his pocket. He was in too much of a hurry, and the object slipped from his fingers, bounced on the sidewalk and came rolling out on the road toward me. Feeling particularly polite at the moment, I hurried to pick it up before Cox got to it and beat him out with inches to spare. I reckon he must have had a guilty conscience or something, because the minute he saw I had it, he backed away to the Apache porch, and his face looked sort of red and white by turns —"

"What was it you picked up?" Nogales asked.

"A cinch ring. And it was pretty well blued from being heated in a brand fire. Anyway, that's how it looked to me —"

"Blued from the heat, eh?" from Caliper. "That sounds like evidence."

"That's the way I looked at it." Tanner nodded. "By the time I was through examining the ring Cox had gone into the Apache. I followed him inside, handed him the ring. Then I asked him direct if it had been used on any of my dogies? You see, I'd heard of some Five-Point-Star critters being sold in the next county, and it sudden occurred to me —"

"— that a Five-Point-Star," Nogales interrupted shrewdly, "could be burned over from a Maple-Leaf. I don't blame you for your suspicions, Tanner. I suppose Cox denied the accusation."

Tanner nodded. "Very emphatically. We called some names back and forth, but he wouldn't go for his iron. Instead, him and Hedge Furlow, who came in while we were talking, put one of the breeds up to picking a fight with me. The breed was too drunk to know he was being used for a cat's paw and he went for his gun. I made a lucky shot and knocked it out of his hand. Then I backed out plenty *pronto,* being as it looked like they'd all gang up on me, which they did. Thinking they had me on the run, they followed me out to the street and — well, about that time you two came along and took a hand, luckily for me."

"We were glad of the chance to help, cowpoke," Nogales said. "So you own the Maple-Leaf outfit, eh? I've heard of that iron."

"You have?" Tanner appeared surprised. "Where did you hear of it?"

Nogales shrugged his shoulders. "Oh, somewhere," he answered vaguely. "I don't remember. . . . You don't happen to have a job for a couple of footloose cow-willies, do you?"

"I wish I had," Tanner replied ruefully, "but I'm paying all the wages I can afford at present. And I don't see any way out of my difficulty. You see, I'm due to lose out if rustlers continue to pick on me as regularly as they have been doing."

Caliper dragged on his cigarette a moment, then said apologetically, "It's none of my business, Tanner, but if you need money to operate, why don't you slap a mortgage on your spread? That'll give you the means to tide you over until the rough spots get smoothed out."

"Exactly what I'd do," Tanner said promptly, "if I owned the Maple-Leaf outright but I don't. I've got a sort of lease from the Southwest Cattle Company, said company being the owners. . . . I've only been here since last June. The Maple-Leaf had a fair herd but no one to handle it. I'm running the outfit. I put my own money into it for running expenses and take a share of the profits — if any. What I'm aiming to do is make enough money to buy the spread outright, if the owners will sell, some time in the future. Either that or get a ranch I can call my own some place else."

Nogales mused. He liked the square-jawed, direct-speaking Tanner. He'd seen him under fire and appreciated his coolness and ability. He knew Caliper was feeling the same way.

"It's this way, Lee," Nogales said at last, "this Caliper maverick is a glutton for work. Me, I'm not so ambitious but I promised him we'd take a job. Now we're both fairly well-heeled at present, so wages don't cut such a big figure with us, being we made a sort of killing on the wheel a spell back. Here's my proposition: we'd like a place to call home for a spell. It's quite possible you can use a couple of extra hands, which same is us. You take us on and we won't talk wages until the Maple-Leaf is in a condition to check off remuneration consistent with responsibility — guess that's good, eh, Caliper?" And Nogales grinned, saying, "And to responsibility I'll add ability, capability and —"

"General debility," Caliper said sarcastically. "I wish you'd quit trying to use big words, Nogales. You make me —"

"Dizzy," Nogales cut in quickly. "Yeah, I've known that for a long time, but Lee understands me, if you don't."

"Who says I don't understand?" Caliper snapped. "To prove that your infinitesimal, insignificant vocabulary hasn't the slightest effect on my gigantic, stupendous, colossal and prodigious mentality, and that I'm the guiding genius of this here two-handed corporation I'm backing your offer. What do you say, Lee?"

Tanner burst out laughing and looked from one to the other. He had to admit that he liked the two strange cowboys, even though they did appear rather crazy at times. He said, "You two sure spread a heap of verbiage when you want to put an idea across, but I gather that you're offering your services, free gratis, until such time as the Maple-Leaf can pay you wages. Well, suppose my outfit turned out to be a failure, what then?"

"We'll chance that," Nogales replied. "I'm used to taking chances, anyway. Got that way riding trails with Caliper. Life may be tough at times, but it's never dull with him siding you."

"Besides," Caliper urged, "we've seen you in action, Lee, and you don't look like a feller who would put money into a losing proposition. I reckon we'd be safe."

Tanner flushed. "Thanks, fellows, I appreciate that." He paused, apparently pondering some question in his mind. Finally he spoke, "Suppose I took you up on your offer, seeing you're both so anxious to go to work — only hired you to somebody else?"

Nogales dragged out tobacco and cigarette papers. He rolled his smoke and lighted up. "Shoot the works, Lee. Our ears are flapping for the story."

"It's this way," Tanner commenced, "the Star-M outfit which adjoins mine is plumb out of luck for help. Old Man Morley used to have a pretty good outfit there, but rustlers just about ruined his herds. The next thing that happened was that Morley was found dead one morning out on the range. He'd been shot in the back."

Caliper swore softly. "So they go in for dry-gulching in this country, too, eh?"

Tanner nodded, saying bitterly, "I told you there was a right lot of scum in these parts. . . . Anyway, Morley's murderer was never discovered. Morley's wife had been dead for years, but his daughter, Lena Lou, was left to run the outfit. The rustlers kept working on her herd — such as was still in existence — until now that's about gone."

"Most ranges," Nogales growled, "the scuts don't pick on women, anyway."

Tanner continued, "Lena Lou isn't the sort to quit when the going gets tough. As she only had a small amount of money she paid off her hands, rather than have them go on and on until finally there wasn't a cent left. She had a certain pride in paying her bills. Then she set out to run the ranch by herself, with only an old Mexican, Pablo Trejos, to help her. Pablo had worked for old Morley for a good many years. He's a white man if there ever was one. Even if Lena Lou had tried to pay him off, he wouldn't have left the outfit."

"I like a man who's loyal thataway," Caliper said.

Tanner nodded. "Anyway, Lena Lou is plumb up against it — just about to the end of her rope. This country, with conditions as they are, is no place for a girl with only old Pablo Trejos for protection. But Lena Lou refuses to leave. I'm worried about the girl. And so I'd appreciate it a heap if you two would hire out to her on the same basis you offered me."

Caliper said, "How about your own outfit?"

"I'm keeping my head above water," Tanner replied. "Lena Lou isn't. She's going down fast and needs help more than I do. I've helped her whenever I could, but she knows my fix and she's plumb independent. She's right, I suppose, when she refuses my help. There wouldn't be much work for you on the Star-M, but decent folks would feel better knowing she had a couple of able-bodied hands out there. In case of trouble old Pablo wouldn't last long. He hasn't the stamina though he'd fight to the last ditch to protect Lena Lou." He paused and looked from one to the other to see how they'd accept the suggestion.

Caliper finished his bottle of beer. "It commences to look, Nogales," he drawled, "like we'd hired out to a female rancher."

Nogales heaved a long sigh. "As that feller Kipling says, 'The female of the species is more ready with the wail!' This here particular wail that Lee mentions falls on my ear. I reckon we're it, Caliper."

"You won't find Lena Lou wailing any," Tanner said quickly.

Caliper grunted skeptically. "Huh! The last petticoat ranch I worked on was run by a lantern-jawed woman with straggly hair, skinny limbs and a razor-blade tongue." He shuddered at the memory. "All right, Tanner, if she'll stand for us, I reckon we can stand her."

"Don't be too sure." Tanner smiled. "We may have to persuade her to take you on. Like I said, she's plumb independent about that matter of paying for what she gets. Anyway, Caliper, I feel Lena Lou Morley won't be quite so difficult to work for as this woman buckaroo you've mentioned."

"She couldn't be," Caliper replied sourly. "Well, let's get started out to this Star-M with its woman boss. I want to see what kind of a bunk I flop into before it gets dark."

A few minutes later the three men mounted and rode out of Orejano. At the edge of town they paused a moment before two trails that forked toward the northwest. Tanner led the way on the right-hand trail. "That other," he explained, "is the road to my ranch, should you ever be coming out from town."

6. Boss of the Circle-Slash

The Star-M Ranch house was a two-story affair of rock and adobe construction. The bunkhouse was a low, squat building, also of adobe, and situated some hundred yards back of the house. The corrals and other smaller miscellaneous buildings were placed in a half-moon formation running to either side of the bunkhouse and a little to the rear. There was some foliage about the grounds: scrub oak, piñon, a bit of mesquite and cottonwoods.

It wasn't much of a ride from Orejano, and the three men arrived shortly before supper time. Lee Tanner led the way past the house to one of the corrals, where saddles were removed and the ponies turned in to mingle with a half-dozen other saddle horses. Then they started back toward the house on foot.

As they approached the house a girl's voice was heard mingling with a man's heavier tones. The next minute the owner of that gruff voice emerged from the door, a look of anger on his heavy, unshaven features. He was a powerfully built individual with bushy eyebrows and a long underlip. A brace of forty-fives hung at his thighs.

"Huh! Two-gun man," Caliper commented.

"He looks like a bad hombre."

"He's an ugly customer," Tanner frowned. "And don't get the idea he can't handle those guns. He's as good with his right hand as his left. I don't know how I've gotten along with him as long as I have."

"Can't say I have any hankerin' to tangle with him," Nogales said slowly, "not unless he forced the issue."

Caliper asked, "Who is he?"

"Straub Krouch," Tanner replied. "He owns the Circle-Slash spread. He also owns the Apache Saloon, which we wrecked this afternoon. I don't think he's going to like that."

Nogales chuckled ruefully. "I'm one dumb lunkhead, I am, if that's the hombre I told the Apache bartender to see me about paying for the smashed mirror and so on. I'm bettin' I've let myself in for some trouble."

They had no time to say more. Straub Krouch was drawing near now on his way to the corral where he'd left his bronc. He glanced up as the three men drew abreast of him.

"H'are you, Krouch?" Tanner said shortly.

"What's it to you?" Krouch snapped irritatedly. He slowed pace and looked at Caliper and Nogales.

Tanner said, "I want you to meet a couple of friends of mine — Nogales Scott and Caliper Maxwell — Straub Krouch."

A sneer formed on Krouch's ugly features as he sized the two cowboys up from head to foot. He made no effort to shake hands. As for Nogales and Caliper, the instant Tanner introduced them they reached for "makin's" to occupy their fingers. They acknowledged the introduction with brief nods. That made things even, though the insolent glances they bestowed on the owner of the Circle-Slash may have given them a slight edge.

"You might as well know it now as any time, Krouch," Lee Tanner said quietly. "We shot up your Apache this afternoon. You'll have a new mirror and some furniture to buy — not to mention bottled stock and glasses —"

"T'hell you say!" Krouch spat. His lips tightened. His hands made an involuntary movement toward guns, then restrained himself. "Who do you mean by — *we* done it?"

"What I said," Tanner replied steadily. "Some of your customers started the trouble, egged on by Hedge Furlow and Stan Cox. Furlow fanned his tail away from the trouble. Nogales, here, presented Cox with a couple of broken arms. Mike Artora will tell you about it when you see him."

Krouch ignored this last. He turned to Nogales, his voice sounding skeptical, "*You* downed *Cox?* Didn't think it could be done in these parts by anybody but me."

"That's probably where you and Cox are in

accord," Nogales drawled. "He didn't figure I could do it, either. Maybe I was just lucky."

"Lucky hell!" Krouch spat. "Luck doesn't work that way against Stan Cox. You must have had something else."

"Uh-huh, I probably did," Nogales admitted carelessly, "— a Colt's forty-five and the ability to use it faster than Cox."

Nogales was fast forming a dislike of Straub Krouch. Well, if they were destined to lock horns, the sooner the better. He continued, "I told your bartender that if you insisted on pay for the damage done, to tell you to come direct to me, and I'd give you what you were looking for." As the words left his lips Nogales tensed, ready for a fast draw.

Krouch noted the slight movement and glared at Nogales a moment. His face grew red, then he relaxed, glaring at the cowboy. Something was warning Krouch to go slow and not press this long, rangy cowpoke too much. That Nogales had downed Cox was giving Krouch food for thought. There was something easygoing about Nogales, but still you could never be certain about that sort of man. Killers had been known to smile even as they pulled trigger. Krouch decided to change his tactics.

"I reckon I can pay for any damage done," he growled. "There ain't any use of you and me tangling — yet."

"Any time you want it," Nogales drawled. "It's up to you, Krouch. I'm not forcing trouble but I'm not running away from it, either."

Krouch ignored this last, asking, "Maybe you two are interested in taking a job. Where did you work last?"

Nogales said, "We haven't worked since early last spring when we pulled out of Wyoming."

Caliper put in, "We got fed up with the tactics of an old miser named Tuck Samson. He was so —"

"Tuck Samson?" Krouch queried. "Up near Cottonwood Center?"

Nogales nodded. "Do you know him?"

"Know him?" Something akin to a smile crossed Krouch's ugly features. "He's my half brother."

"Then you know," Caliper said belligerently, "that Samson is so tight the eagle screams every time he closes his hand on a dollar. He holds it so tight that by the time the dollar leaves his hand it's worth only fifty cents!"

"You can't tell me anything about Tuck Samson," Krouch growled. "He backed me in my operations down here."

"He backed you?" Nogales said in amazement. "I can't imagine anybody getting money out of Samson."

"He's backing me," Krouch explained, "because he knows I always make money. I'm payin' better than ten per cent on the loan, and Samson gets a share in the profits. I'm always getting letters demandin' that I make more money."

"Then," Nogales said thoughtfully, "if you don't make money, neither does Tuck Samson?"

"That's about the size of it. And if my business ever failed — which it won't — he'd lose money."

"Very, very interestin'," Caliper murmured.

Krouch frowned. "Someday I'll get squared around and make enough money to pay him off in a lump sum. Then I won't have the miserly old buzzard on my shoulders all the time. . . . What are you two fellers doing down here? Are you interested in taking jobs?"

Nogales shook his head emphatically. "Nope, we wouldn't crave to punch for anybody that's got the same blood in his veins as Tuck Samson — if it is blood. I always had an idea it was ice water to tell the truth —"

"Now don't get me wrong," Krouch broke in. "Anybody that works for me draws good wages." He frowned at the derisive sound from Lee Tanner's direction and went on, "I've got a good cook, and my hands eat the best. I even pay a mite extra sometimes for good work —"

"You're too late, Krouch," Nogales said. "I reckon we've got jobs."

"What!" Krouch looked amazed. He shot out the next two words. "Who with?"

"The Star-M. We haven't seen our boss yet, but Tanner has it all fixed up."

Krouch whirled on Tanner. "These two old friends of yours, Tanner?"

Tanner laughed shortly. "I never saw 'em before today," he said truthfully. "They horned in to help me out at the Apache."

"Strangers, eh?" Krouch rasped. He swung back to Nogales and Caliper. "Ten to one Tanner hasn't told you that the Star-M is on its last legs. Lena Lou Morley can't afford to pay wages. If you want to go to work for me, I'll pay you genuine money — not promises." His voice took on a meaning tone. "Maybe if you're top hands and know your business you could draw down a bonus on the side."

Caliper said innocently, "I'm afraid we wouldn't do. We're no good at blanket work."

"Blanket work!" Krouch's face flamed. "Who said anything about brand-blotting?"

"Nobody," Nogales replied promptly. "Caliper was just telling you, so you wouldn't think we were the ones who were doing all the rustling in these parts that Tanner has been telling us about. We're strangers here and don't aim to get into trouble through folks suspicioning us, like they have at other places we've worked at in the past. Caliper

85

has a sort of guilty conscience that works overtime on occasion."

Straub Krouch placed his own interpretation on the words — exactly as Caliper and Nogales had intended he should. For the first time Krouch really smiled. He felt sure now that these two strange cowboys would fit into his schemes. Before committing himself, however, he wanted to know more about them. "Well," he said, "I've offered you a job, with pay — which same is more than Lena Lou Morley can do. Come out to my Circle-Slash some time, or I'll meet you at the Apache in town, and we'll talk it over."

"Can't Miss Morley pay us wages?" Caliper asked, astonishment written all over his round face.

"Hell, no!" Krouch growled. "She hasn't any money."

Nogales burst out, "This is a hell of a note." He turned angrily on the amazed Lee Tanner. "Looks like to me, Tanner, as if you gave us a bum steer," he accused in hurt tones. "After we helped you out of a fight, I felt we could take your word for things. How about that legacy that you said Miss Morley had inherited? Were you just ribbing us?"

"Yeah," Caliper put in hotly, "that's a fine way to treat a feller. You said Miss Morley had money to burn. Those were your exact words!"

Tanner stared at the two in sudden confusion, swept off his feet by the strange accusations. "There must be some mistake, fellows," he said earnestly. "I didn't say anything like that. I — I don't see where you ever got such an impression."

"Well, that's what you told us," Nogales snapped. "Didn't he, Caliper?"

"He sure did." Caliper nodded emphatically.

Straub Krouch looked keenly at Tanner and noted the man's flustered manner, which was so genuine that Krouch got the impression, then and there, that Tanner was trying to conceal some secret from him.

"How about it, Tanner?" Krouch demanded crisply. "Has Lena Lou come into some money recent?"

"Not — not that I know of," Tanner stammered in reply, looking bewildered.

Krouch sneered. "Rats! You're not so good at keeping secrets as you should be, Tanner. You can't lie to me. I'm not believing you." He whirled contemptuously away from Tanner and faced the two punchers. "Nogales, you and Caliper come to see me when you want a job. I'll raise any figure the Star-M offers you."

With that he whirled away and continued on toward the corral. The three men watched him lead out his horse and saddle it, then leap into the saddle and ride off.

Lee Tanner stared after him a moment,

then swung angrily on Nogales and Caliper. "Dammit!" Lee said with considerable irritation. "What made you fellows say that? Were you trying to force Krouch to raise his price?"

Nogales and Caliper had been trying to keep straight faces. Now they laughed outright at Tanner's manner. Tanner disgustedly turned away and started for the house. Nogales and Caliper hurried to catch up.

"Don't get us wrong, Lee," Nogales said, grinning. "Hell! I wouldn't work for that bustard if he offered me a gold mine. I was just putting out a few feelers to see how he'd take 'em."

Tanner heaved a long, relieved sigh. "I'm danged if I know what to think of you two. You sure had me worried for a minute. Sometimes I think maybe you're cracked —"

"Nogales is," Caliper chuckled promptly.

"Take a feller like Caliper," Nogales flashed, "and he doesn't have any head to crack. His skull is as empty as last year's birds' nests. . . . But it's this way, Lee, we were just running a little bluff on Krouch. If he thinks the Star-M has money it won't surprise him so much if we take jobs with it. It would look plumb fishy if he thought we were going to work for nothing, and he might start getting cautious. I don't want him changing his ways a bit. One way or another I'm going to get Straub Krouch just where I want him."

"And by taking a fall out of Krouch," Caliper grinned, "we'll also be hurting Tuck Samson in a fatal spot — his pocketbook. My, oh, my!"

"And here's another slant, Lee," Nogales went on. "We've already got Krouch to thinking we have shady reputations. I wouldn't be surprised if he'd spill something to one of us someday — something that you might never get wind of. Do you get what we're working toward?"

Tanner looked at the two with undisguised admiration. "I never did see a pair work together like you two do," he said. "The two of you are just like a well-oiled machine."

"I saw Nogales once when he was well oiled," Caliper chuckled, "but he wasn't any machine. He couldn't hardly move as a matter of fact. What a hang-over!"

"What I'm getting at," Tanner smiled, "is that you two aren't so dumb at that."

"One of us isn't, you mean," Nogales put in. "I always have to do the thinking for both."

"And look where your thinking got us," Caliper jeered. "Here we are, two able-bodied top hands working on a petticoat outfit run by a gal and an old Mexican."

Nogales laughed. "The funniest part is we're doing it without wages. If Tuck Samson ever hears of such a condition pervailing down here, I'll bet he moves his outfit, lock, stock and barrel, and picks himself up some daughters and an old Mexican!"

7. Plain Robbery

By this time the three men had reached the ranch house. Lena Lou Morley met them at the back door. She was a tall, pretty girl with black hair, lovely brown eyes and a very determined chin. She was clad in mannish flannel shirt, corduroy divided skirt and riding boots. At her right hip hung a holstered six-shooter, which she was at that moment removing.

Nogales looked into her eyes and was lost forever. So, too, Caliper. Tanner performed the introductions, and the two cowboys were rewarded with firm grasps of the girl's cool, slim hand.

"You're just in time to have supper with me," Lena Lou invited in her full, throaty voice. "It would have been on the table now, except that Straub Krouch held me up with his talk." Her dark eyes flashed angrily. "The nerve of the man! He rode in here and unsaddled his bronc and put it in the corral as though he was going to stay all afternoon." She laughed suddenly. "I guess he did, almost. Dang him, anyway. Sometimes I almost hate that man."

"Caliper and I have decided the same

thing," Nogales said. "To me he looks snaky bad, Miss Morley."

"Make it plain Lena Lou," the girl cut in. "That's what everybody calls me — friends and foes alike. I hope you're not going to be foes, though." Then to Tanner, "What did Krouch have to say, Lee? Come inside and talk while I get supper on the table."

Tanner told first how he had met Caliper and Nogales, then of their offer to work for the Star-M. Lastly he related the conversation they'd had with Straub Krouch. The girl nodded from time to time but made no comments while she busied herself with the supper things at the stove in the kitchen. The cowboys went to wash up, then returned to the house. At last everything was on the table and ready to be eaten. There were hot biscuits, chicken, potatoes, gravy, pie and coffee.

Tanner looked at the feast in astonishment. "Gosh, Lena Lou," he exclaimed, "where did you get the chicken?"

Lena Lou laughed. "Pablo brought it to me this morning. I didn't ask where he'd got it. He'd been visiting nearby relatives, so I suppose one of his many in-laws is shy one fat hen. Pablo's a wonder that way, and it sure helps out." She turned to Caliper and Nogales. "Pablo is my foreman, Pablo Trejos. He's the only man I have here. He's been loyal to the Star-M for years and years."

"Yes ma'am." Nogales nodded. "Lee was

91

telling us about him." Caliper's mouth was too full of food for comment.

So far the girl hadn't commented on the two cowboys' offer of their services. Finally, when the meal was finished and cigarettes were being rolled, she got down to business.

"A few days ago," she commenced, "I wouldn't have thought of taking you men on without paying you wages, but I've changed my mind now. I'll be right glad to have you here — as long as you'll stay."

"Why the sudden decision?" Nogales asked.

"Krouch!" she answered somewhat angrily. "He's been riding out here one day each week trying to persuade me to sell the Star-M to him. Today he was unusually persistent. When I refused to sell today, as I always do, he figured another way to get control of this outfit."

"The same being?" Caliper asked.

Lena Lou smiled contemptuously. "He asked me to marry him and acted quite upset when I laughed in his face at the proposition. Ugh! Marry that beast!"

Tanner started up from his chair, swearing oaths under his breath. "I'll fix that low-down coyote —" he commenced.

"Sit down, Lee!" the girl spoke swiftly. "You'll do nothing of the sort. I'm much obliged just the same but I intend to fight my own battles. You just 'tend to your Maple-Leaf and you'll have your hands full without taking on any of my grievances. Now maybe I will sell just to get rid of Krouch."

"Why not, if you can get a good price for the outfit?" Caliper asked.

"That's the rub," Lena Lou answered wryly. "Krouch won't pay a decent price. In its present condition I'll admit that the value of the Star-M is away below par, but Krouch won't even pay what it's worth. He probably figures to get it the same way he did the Circle-Slash, and that was a steal if there ever was one, I —"

"Excuse me, Lena Lou," Nogales cit in, "but just how did he get the Circle-Slash?"

Lena Lou explained. "Six months ago the Circle-Slash was in the same condition the Star-M is now. Little by little its herds had dwindled away — the result of rustling, of course. Krouch made its owner an offer that made the deal plain robbery, but the owner was glad to get anything out of it he could. He never did have much backbone, that fellow. Anyway, he let it go for a fraction of its worth. Krouch paid cash on the nail and immediately commenced to replenish the stock. Right now Straub Krouch is on the road to becoming rather an influential figure in cattle circles hereabouts. I suppose he plans to work the same scheme with the Star-M. If he can get my Star-M, I'll bet he goes after the Maple-Leaf next, then you'll have to look out, Lee. He'll rob you blind if you let him. Of course he can't very well get the deed to the property, with that being held by the Southwest Cattle Company, but what he could do to your herds is a shame."

"You're not telling me anything new," Tanner said seriously. He turned to Caliper and Nogales. "It may be that Krouch is leading the rustlers in this vicinity, but I haven't been able to get any real proof of that yet. I've tried to keep an eye on him, but the Maple-Leaf takes all my time as a rule. I don't get a chance to ride around as much as I'd like. You see, I've got to cut the buck or lose my money and the confidence of the Southwest Cattle Company."

Lena Lou nodded. "That's the situation. Neither of us have the time to trail around looking for rustler evidence and we can't afford to hire men to do it for us. We haven't a thing against Krouch, actually. I just feel he's back of the move to swindle us. What I want to make clear is" — speaking to Nogales and Caliper — "if you two men hire on with me you've a very slim chance of ever getting your money. There isn't much to be done around here any more, so your work would probably consist of looking for rustlers. I don't need to tell you that is risky sometimes —"

"We understand that, all the way through, Lena Lou," Nogales cut in. "There's a lot of painting and repairing needed here, but for the present we'll forget that and take care of what stock is left —"

"If you can find it," Lena Lou said with dry humor.

Nogales nodded. "Anyway, I've got an idea —"

Caliper interrupted. "Now there's something to marvel at — Nogales with an idea —"

"— but I'm not ready to say what it is," Nogales finished smoothly as though he hadn't heard the interruption. "First, where does Krouch's Circle-Slash lie?"

"Over south of my place," Tanner said. "The Maple-Leaf is just midway between the Circle-Slash and the Star-M."

"I'll be looking over his place within the next two-three days maybe," Nogales said. "If I meet Krouch in town maybe I'll talk to him a mite. He might drop something by accident he hadn't intended to drop."

At that moment a lean, leathery, wrinkled Mexican with gray hair entered the room. He stopped at sight of the two strangers, but Lena Lou bade him stay. "Pablo, we're taking on two hands — Nogales and Caliper. I think they're going to help us a heap."

Pablo smiled and shook hands with the two punchers. Both liked him at sight. Old he may have been but he was as straight as an arrow, and his eyes were young under the snow-white brows.

"The supper things are still warm, Pablo," Lena Lou said. "Did you hear anything while you were away?"

The old Mexican's face suddenly grew grave. "Thee ghost herd has been seen again, señorita — last night!"

A look of impatience crossed Lena Lou's features. "Oh pshaw! Pablo! That's all nonsense. Ghosts don't exist."

The old man drew up in dignity. "I myself saw eet two months back, señorita. Last evening my cousin, Pedro Contortez, was returning home from Mexico and he saw the herd —"

Nogales cut in, "What's this ghost herd you're talking about?"

Pablo shrugged his shoulders. "The Americano talk I do not handle well, señor. It is bes' the Señorita Lena Lou tell you of the ghost herd. I weel go to get my supper."

He stalked out of the dining room, headed for the kitchen.

Lena Lou laughed when the old Mexican had disappeared. "There, I've offended his dignity again. . . . Of course there isn't anything to this ghost herd he speaks of. That is simply one of the many superstitions of the Mexicans in these parts. You know how they are."

Nogales nodded. "Some of 'em put a heap of faith in this supernatural stuff," he agreed. "Have you or Lee ever seen this ghost herd Pablo speaks of?"

Both the girl and Tanner shook their heads. "Neither of us ever took any stock in the story," Lena Lou said, "so we never went over to Phantom Pass to investigate. These Mexicans probably see shadows or something of the sort and think they are seeing ghosts."

"What kind of a ghost is it supposed to be?" Caliper wanted to know. "Where's Phantom Pass?"

Lena Lou explained. "Phantom Pass is over the other side of the Circle-Slash Ranch. You've probably noticed that this country hereabouts is pretty well hedged in by mountain range. Well, Phantom Pass is a narrow, high-walled canyon that runs right through the chain of mountains to the Mexican Border and into the country to the south beyond."

Lee Tanner expanded on the subject. "You see, unless we go way round, Phantom Pass is the only trail through to Mexico. Near the entrance to the pass — on the United States side — is an old adobe house now pretty much in ruins. At least it was the last time I saw it, which is some time ago. The tale goes that an old Mexican named Constado used to live there. It seems one night when he was driving a herd through to Mexico someone shot and killed him, then ran off with the cows. . . . Within the past year the ghost of Constado and his phantom herd are said to have been seen, several times. The Mexicans

97

hereabouts claim the pass is haunted, and you can't hire them to go near it at night."

"It all sounds very silly to me." Lena Lou smiled.

Nogales nodded. "Yes, it does. But some folks are always getting ideas about spooks and such."

He asked a few more questions about the location of Phantom Pass and mentioned that he'd like to go ghost hunting some time when the present trouble was ended. In time the subject was changed.

The three men and the girl sat talking until after eight o'clock. Tanner told how he had scoured the country in the hope of finding some of his cows with changed brands but without success. A little after eight o'clock he rose and said good night. Getting his horse, he mounted and rode off toward his Maple-Leaf Ranch.

After Tanner had left, Nogales and Caliper bade Lena Lou good-night and went down to the bunkhouse, where they found old Pablo braiding a horsehair quirt. They tried to draw the old Mexican into a discussion of the Phantom Pass and its ghost herd, but Pablo was reluctant to talk of the matter, a certain look of fear entering his eyes when the subject was mentioned. When he finally and with considerable courtesy, announced that he was going to get into his bunk for the night the two cowboys realized they'd get nothing out of him. They both followed Pablo's example and, crawling between blankets, were soon fast asleep.

8. The Ghost Herd

How long they'd been asleep Caliper didn't know when he was awakened by Nogales. Caliper, his eyes hardly open, sat up, reached for his sombrero and commenced to roll a cigarette.

"Shhh! You warp-legged cow-nurse," Nogales whispered. "Don't make so much noise. You'll wake the old Mex."

"What's the idea?" Caliper whispered back, getting his eyes open. Pale moonlight filtered through a window in the bunkhouse. In one of the other bunks they could hear Pablo snoring peacefully. After a minute Caliper made out that Nogales was fully dressed. "Where we going?" Caliper asked. He commenced to pull on his boots.

"We're going for a little ride," Nogales replied in low tones. "Hurry up."

Without another word Caliper finished dressing, buckled on his gun and fumbled around in the dark for his saddle.

"Bring your rifle too," Nogales advised.

Neither spoke again until their ponies had been saddled and they had mounted and were well away from the ranch buildings. The two cowboys rode on in silence for some time, Caliper waiting for his companion to explain the reason for the sudden awakening and departure from the Star-M.

Finally, looking up at the moon, which was partly under a cloud by this time, Caliper ventured, "It'll be midnight in another hour."

"Thanks for the information," Nogales returned dryly. "I was just thinking about that — and some other things."

Caliper spurred his horse closer. "Yeah? What was you thinking about? That a night ride of this kind is good for your complexion or something? Or did you think the broncs needed a workout? Just full of information you are."

"I was thinking," Nogales stated, taking a certain amusement in keeping Caliper guessing, "that Lena Lou is plumb ornamental — and what terrible table manners you have."

"Terrible manners I have!" Caliper blurted in surprise. "Now what the blasted Hades have I been doing? What's wrong with my table manners?"

"It was that terrible fox paw you made at supper," Nogales explained gravely.

"Fox paw! Are you crazy? We haven't seen any foxes since we left Wyoming —"

"You idiot," Nogales said disgustedly. "I was just airing my French. *F-a-u-x p-a-s*, fox paw. It means 'mistake' in the French language. Don't you remember we learned that when we were in Chicago?"

Caliper's brow cleared. "Oh, you mean fox pass! I get you. Airing your French, eh? Cowpoke, it needs airing. It smells right bad, if you ask me. So far as that goes, anything *you* say in any language means 'mistake'. . . . Well, what mistake did I make at supper?"

Nogales shook his head scornfully. "Mistakes, not mistake. But I can't remember 'em all. One of the worst was drinking your coffee out of your saucer thataway."

"But it was hot."

"That's no excuse. It looked like you didn't know any etiquette. Even if it was hot, you should still drink out of your cup."

"No siree!" Caliper shook his head. "You don't catch me drinking out of a cup again. Last time I tried that I stuck the spoon handle in my eye."

To this Nogales made no answer. He was again deep in thought. The two horses pounded on across the range. Now and then Nogales glanced around to keep his direction straight but he had little to say, nor could Caliper draw him into conversation for some time.

Finally Caliper ventured, "Look here, Nogales, I don't mind being woke up out of a sound sleep, but I don't see any fun in tearing off across the range this way unless I know what it's all about. I'll back your hunches from hell to breakfast but I figure you should let me know what's on your mind. You know ruddy well you didn't bring me 'way out here to lecture me on table etiquette. Or if you did, we're both suckers. Me for coming and you for wasting time."

Nogales was suddenly contrite. "Excuse it, old hawss. My mind's so full of ideas that I can't think proper. I should have told you before. . . . We're riding over to Phantom Pass and see if the ghost herd walks tonight."

Caliper's face brightened. "Suffering rattlesnake puppies! Do you think there's something queer about that, too? It looked plumb crazy to me. Cowboy, I'm with you! Lena Lou and Tanner just laughed off the story, but Mexicans can think as well as the next man. Where there's so much smoke there must be some fire. Do you think we'll find anything in the ghost line?" he finished eagerly.

Nogales shrugged his muscular shoulders. "I haven't the least idea. Either there's something scaring hell out of a heap of Mexican folks, or old Pablo's a liar. And I figure him as a straight shooter. He's lived too long on the Morley ranch to be deceived by a bunch of superstitions. Come on, let's shake these broncs up a mite."

They put spurs to the ponies and increased speed. For two hours they rode steadily across rolling grasslands. Occasionally the horses were allowed to slow to a walk to gain a second wind — then spurs, and the animals lengthened strides again. They had passed within a half mile of Tanner's place some time before. Lights in the bunkhouse windows told them Tanner or some of his hands were still up.

"Probably Lee," Nogales mused. "I bet he gives a heap of time that should be spent sleeping in trying to solve all his problems."

The horses drummed on through the night. Eventually they followed a trail running past a group of dark buildings. "Krouch's hangout," Nogales called to Caliper through the rush of wind that beat past their faces. "Looks like he's got quite a prosperous place there."

Caliper nodded. Within a few minutes the Krouch ranch was left to the rear.

Gradually the ponies commenced to ascend rising ground. Clumps of brush and trees were passed. The way became more rocky, and the horses were forced to slow speed a trifle. Finally a long, dark ridge showed ahead.

Nogales signaled to his companion, and the two drew rein. It wasn't yet three o'clock in the morning.

"We're on the right trail," Nogales said. "There's the hogback that Lena Lou mentioned. We should be able to see Phantom Pass from the top of that ridge."

At the foot of the hogback they dismounted and, after tethering their mounts in the brush, made their way on foot to the top. It was a stiffish climb, burdened with rifles as they were, but the crest was finally reached by the two heavily breathing cow-punchers.

They threw themselves flat on the earth at the top of the ridge and peered about, trying to locate Phantom Pass. Caliper was first to spot the entrance to the canyon. "There it is," he said to Nogales, "— no, over to the right more. See it now? There's the two tall rocks at the entrance that Lena Lou told us about. You can see the break in the mountains."

"I see it." Nogales nodded. He glanced at the sky. "We'll be able to see better in a minute when the moon comes all the way out from under that cloud."

Within a few minutes the scene brightened. There, something over a quarter of a mile away, Phantom Pass was plainly visible to the two cowboys. They couldn't mistake the spot now, so accurate had been Lena Lou's description. A short distance to the right of the entrance to the pass they could distinguish the square, squat outlines of an old adobe house. The scene was all clear now, but there wasn't a movement to be seen about the place. It looked as though it had been deserted for years. When the moonlight brightened, Nogales could even make out a spot at one corner where the wall was crumbling away. It was a desolate-looking ruin, a fit setting for the tale that had grown up about it.

"Do you suppose Constado's ghost is in there now?" Caliper asked.

"Who's Constado?"

"You know, the Mex that was killed when he was herding his cows through the pass. It's his ghost —"

"Sure enough. I'd forgotten the name for a moment. I was thinking about something else."

Caliper laughed softly. "I was just wondering, if Constado's ghost comes out of that house will he be walking or riding? Or maybe he might chop some wood for a change." He laughed again as though to reassure himself. "You know, that place sort of gets to a feller in spite of himself. Course I never did believe any of these stories you hear about haunted houses. At the same time you get to wondering sometimes."

Nogales nodded soberly. "It's right spooky looking, especially when you remember that murder was done there. Look at those fallen trees near the house, left to rot. Gosh, it's mighty lonesome looking down there."

Caliper's voice sounded rather small when he spoke next. "Of course I don't know everything and —"

"I'll say you don't."

"No fooling now, Nogales," Caliper said a

bit irritatedly. "But I was just thinking, we laugh at ghost stories and so on, but there's lots of things people don't know nor understand. Suppose there really were ghosts in the world? Some pretty well educated people claim to have seen 'em. Maybe they're right and we're wrong."

"You mean maybe there really are ghosts?"

"Yes, for all we know — for certain —"

"I don't want to believe anything like that."

"Me, neither, but — what would you do right now if a ghost walked up to you?"

Nogales pondered a moment. "I don't know. Shake hands and invite him to have a drink maybe."

Somehow it didn't sound very funny right then. The wind had come up a little and was moaning eerily through the trees in the hollow below. There was something ghastly, unreal, in the pale light of the moon. Somewhere in the hills a coyote howled, and the cry echoed weirdly among the rocks until the last echo had died to a whispering silence.

"My Gawd," Caliper muttered, "I don't blame some of these Mexes for getting scared. That wind sounds plumb mournful. Do you know, I hate to admit it but I'm just as glad I'm not any nearer than this to that 'dobe house down there."

"Don't let your imagination run away with you, cowboy."

"I'm not, Nogales, but you've got to admit

it's mighty scarylike. Do you think there's a skeleton and clanking chains in that house down there? Those things always go with haunted houses."

Nogales laughed nervously. "Shut up, will you? Do you want to give me the creeps?" He added after a minute, "You aren't scared, are you?"

Caliper shivered, his teeth chattering a little. "Nope — no more than you are," he taunted. "It's the chill breeze that's making me shake like this."

"Uh-huh, cowboy," Nogales said, gulping a little, "I know just how you feel. No matter how much we reason things out and laugh at superstitions; still we can't ever be sure but what there might be *something* —"

A sudden gasp left Caliper's lips: "Good God! Look at that!"

Nogales caught his breath at what he saw down below. "The ghost herd!" he exclaimed shakily.

The moon was partly hidden by a cloud, but they could see plainly the ghostly figure of a steer at one corner of the old adobe house! Another animal followed behind and a third. Others moved slowly into view, until a small bunch of about twenty ghostly white animals had formed suddenly before their very eyes!

Beads of sweat stood out on Caliper's fore-head, but he retained enough presence of mind to lift his rifle to his shoulder. The barrel wobbled about uncertainly, as his finger sought the trigger.

Nogales restrained him. "Wait," he whispered hoarsely, "don't do that. You're too far away for good shooting. Wait, and let's see what happens."

"I know I'm a rotten shot with a rifle," Caliper muttered between his teeth, trying to keep them from chattering, "but I think I could make it. I'll wait, though." He lowered the rifle with trembling hands.

The two cowboys lay there motionless, eyes glued on the phantom herd below, as it moved around the corner of the old adobe house. And then at the tail end of the herd *appeared a horseman!*

"Constado's ghost!" Nogales gasped, eyes staring at the specter.

Speechless now, the two cowboys gazed, wide-eyed and bewildered, while the ghostly procession slowly wended its way past the adobe house and progressed toward the entrance of Phantom Pass. . . . Suddenly, one by one, the cattle faded from view as they drew near the pass.

Nogales blinked his eyes, trying to make himself believe that what he saw wasn't true. Cattle just couldn't disappear in such fashion. Caliper, at his side, was muttering crazily, watching the same phenomenon.

One by one the cattle vanished. Left now

was only the apparition of the horseman. Abruptly, even while the cowboys watched, breathless, the horseman threw both hands in the air and toppled forward from his mount as though he had been shot, though not a sound except the eerily moaning wind in the trees, had been heard. Even as he fell, horse and rider seemed to melt into the atmosphere. In a moment all was as before.

Somewhere on a distant hill a coyote's mournful howl drifted across the uncanny silence. The moon sifted behind a cloud. . . .

9. "Keep a Loose Holster!"

Nogales and Caliper heaved a deep sigh, stared awe-stricken at one another. Both directed their gaze toward Phantom Pass. Everything looked as it had before the appearance of the ghostly procession. The two cowboys exchanged sickly grins. Nogales strained his eyes for fully five minutes. He could hear Caliper breathing heavily beside him. Nothing more came into view. Nogales rubbed his eyes and turned to his pardner. "Caliper, did you see what I saw? Are we both going plumb cuckoo? Did we really see ghosts, or was it our imagination? I want to know!"

Caliper forced a thin laugh. "I saw it! What do you reckon it is? I still can't believe there's real ghosts in the world."

"If they're real they're not ghosts," Nogales said with a touch of humor that didn't quite come off. "But you've got me; I don't understand it. You and I aren't the type to be frightened off like superstitious folks, neither. Howsomever, I'm admitting, without any urging, that act was plumb spooky. And I don't mean maybe, pard."

"Whoever is back of it," Caliper said soberly, "stages it mighty scary — *look, pard, there it is again!*"

Pale moonlight drifted across the scene as the ghostly herd once more commenced its march from around the corner of the adobe house. One by one the cows passed as before across the astonished gaze of the two punchers. The phantom rider again rode at the tail of the herd, moving with silent, solemn gait that made him appear to float in thin air. Then, a second time, while the cowboys watched, the leading cows commenced to vanish. One by one they faded from view, until only the ghost herdsman was left.

"This time," Caliper muttered, "I aim to do something about him. . . ." Without waiting to complete the sentence, Caliper jerked his Winchester to shoulder . . . pressed trigger . . . fired!

The shot echoed and re-echoed across the hills. The phantom rider stiffened suddenly, then drove in his spurs and rode frantically for cover. In an instant he was behind the 'dobe house, and there was no sign left of cows or rider.

"Wow, cowboy!" Nogales exclaimed, "that threw a scare into 'em. I reckon they're not ghosts after all."

Caliper grinned with sheepish relief. "Mister, I'm commencing to feel a heap better. That danged business was getting me down. I was beginning to think my mind was playing me tricks."

"You and me both." Nogales nodded.

"I reckon I missed with that shot so far as a target is concerned," Caliper said, "but it sure got results — hey, where you going?"

Nogales was already sliding down the steep bank of the hogback. "Don't stand up," he said swiftly, "those hombres might have some good shots among 'em, and you'd make a *buen* mark to pick off. We don't know how many there are at that 'dobe house. They're going to come to investigate right sudden. We'd be outnumbered perhaps. Come on, let's fan tail out of here before they start chasing us. Move, cowboy, move!"

And move Caliper did. He came sliding down beside Nogales in a shower of dried, broken-off branches and dust. In a moment they had reached the bottom. Another instant and they were up, racing toward their waiting horses, vaulting into saddles and using spurs.

The two rode furiously for an hour without stopping or speaking. Finally, when the horses commenced to show palpable signs of weakening, they pulled to a halt. They listened intently, but if there had been any sort of pursuit it must have been abandoned. They could hear nothing from the back trail. By now the moon had dropped beneath the horizon, and, although a few stars still shone in the velvety blackness overhead, a faint streak of gray light — false dawn — was commencing to show in the east.

For another hour the two loped along. Flaming dawn melted the stars from the night. Morning arrived in a blaze of heat and cloudless blue sky. The horses were traveling at an easy, running walk now.

Nogales reined his pony nearer Caliper's. "Did you ever stop to think — ?" he commenced.

"Nope," Caliper interrupted with a grin, "I don't have to stop to think — thinking is a habit with me that comes natural."

"— that the ghost herd is all a put-up job," Nogales continued imperturbably, "to keep folks away from Phantom Pass at night?"

"What do you mean?" Caliper asked curiously.

"Suppose you were a rustler and had some stock to dispose of in Mexico. Say you had a steady market for stolen stuff across the line and didn't have to give a thought to selling stuff in the states. How would you get your cows across?"

Caliper pondered this for a moment. "Why, if I was working this section of the country I'd have to drive 'em through Phantom Pass. Lena Lou said that was the only way to get to Mexico from this neck of the range, unless you took a roundabout trail circling the mountains."

"Exactly. I think that's what's happening.

Tanner told us he had scoured the country for changed brands. Now, Tanner isn't any fool but he couldn't find any. That means, I think, there weren't any to find. The reason for that is the rustlers change the brands, keep the cows hid out until the brands have healed, then drive 'em over into *mañana* land — traveling through Phantom Pass."

"Maybe you're right — but what's all that got to do with those ghosts we saw?"

"Cowboy," Nogales remarked unfeelingly, "you're so dumb you still don't realize there was a Civil War fought in this country a spell back —"

"Don't see how the opposing factions could be 'civil' and still fight a 'war.' "

"Skip it, smart aleck. What I'm getting at, if you were driving stolen cows through Phantom Pass pretty regularly, you wouldn't want strangers stumbling on your activities by accident, would you? Well, then, the thing to do is keep 'em away. You can't put up a sign warning against trespassing because you don't own Phantom Pass; 'sides, it would look queer if you did and —"

"I get you, I get you!" Caliper cried excitedly. "Therefore, the next best thing is to throw a scare into folks, so they'll keep clear of the pass at night of their own accord. Whether they believe in ghosts or not, most folks don't want to go riding through a country where ghosts are supposed to be seen ever so often. There's something about spooky nights that folks fight shy of."

"So the idea finally filtered into your noodle-soup brain, did it?" Nogales said sarcastically. "Sure, you get the idea. There can't be any other explanation, as I see it. Mostly, they're Mexicans in this part of the country and plumb superstitious. The Americano cowmen aren't going to ride clear over to the pass to investigate ghost stories that they don't take any stock in, anyway. The rustlers, knowing the Mexicans' weakness for ghosts, play up that yarn about Constado being murdered and how he rides every night and so on. A few Mexicans, being braver than the rest, ride over to look into the story, maybe. The rustlers put on that ghost parade nearly every night, ten to one, and the Mexes, seeing it, believe it is God's own work. After that they keep plumb away from Phantom Pass and tell their friends to do likewise. Meanwhile the stolen cattle are run across the line, through the pass, without interference."

"By golly!" Caliper exclaimed. "I believe you've hit it, Nogales. Maybe when there's a bunch of stolen cows ready to be put through the pass, the rustlers put on that ghost procession for several nights previous, thus scaring off anybody that might be around at the time."

"That's it. And it looks like the scheme has

sure been successful."

"What I don't understand," Caliper frowned, "is what makes that herd and rider look like ghosts. Gosh, it almost seemed like I could see right through 'em. I could almost swear I saw one of those cows pass completely through some brush once without even disturbing the branches."

"It's queer all right," Nogales pondered. "They've got something that fools us into thinking we see something we don't. It's some sort of optical illusion, I'm betting, that wouldn't fool us a minute if we could see it up close. We'll find out how it's done one of these days — or nights — if we live long enough. The main thing is that we've proved to ourselves that they ain't ghosts."

"But how do they do it?"

"You got me," Nogales admitted. "Anyway, you're in too much of a rush to learn everything at once. Hold your hawsses, waddie. Don't forget that Rome the books tell about, wasn't built in a day."

"No, but it burnt all to hell in one night," Caliper retorted. "Me, I'm honin' for action, now that I've discovered powder smoke can have an effect on a ghost." He chuckled, "Gosh! How that phantom rider did tear for cover!"

"I don't blame you for being curious about the whole business. I am, too. But first I'd like to learn who's backing the rustlers —

who's behind 'em. It's the leader we got to get our claws on. Once we've got him, then the other stuff will come clear. Meanwhile let's not mention to anybody what we've learned about the ghost herd."

They rode on and within a short time reached the Star-M Ranch. The sun was climbing fast by this time. In the ranch yard they met Lena Lou.

"So you haven't run away after all?" she smiled. "Pablo came up and said you weren't in your bunks when he awakened. Where have you been?"

"Well, it's like this, Lena Lou," Nogales explained gravely. "Caliper had the nightmare bad last night, so we saddled up and took the mare out to break her and —"

"Being as she was a nightmare," Caliper joined in, "we had to let her go, come morning. She just vanished sort of. And here we are, hungry as a couple of lobos in fly time —"

Lena Lou's laugh interrupted their story. "Be sensible, boys. I asked where you'd been. I'm too old to believe in fairy stories, you know."

"To tell the truth, Lena Lou," Nogales started again, "we never do sleep well the first night in a strange bunkhouse. So we got up early and took a little ride just to look over the range a mite."

Lena Lou eyed him steadily. "All right,

that's your story and you're stuck with it. What you call getting up early may have something to do with the horses I heard leaving some time before midnight last night. But I won't ask any more questions if you're not ready to tell me where you were. I'll learn in your own good time, I suppose."

"Well, to tell the truth, Lena Lou," Nogales commenced, "we rode over to Phantom Pass to see if we could find the ghost herd."

"And did you?" the girl asked, her eyes sparkling.

"We sure did," Caliper put in. "There was that ghost herd and the ghost of old Constado riding along behind. And they just melted into the brush all of a sudden — disappeared plumb before our eyes —"

Lena Lou burst into sudden laughter. "Go along with you," she said. "Didn't I tell you I was too old to believe in fairy stories? You two are hopeless! I never will believe a word you tell me until you come down to earth and talk sense. Go on up to the house and eat your breakfast. Pablo's there now. I'll be in in a couple of minutes."

Nogales and Caliper continued on toward the house. Caliper said ruefully, "Isn't that just like a woman? Even when you tell 'em the truth, they think you're holding out on 'em. It must be they take it for granted that all men are liars."

"It's just as well," Nogales nodded seriously, "if she doesn't know what we've discovered. She might say something to Pablo and the news would get around. I'd like to keep it quiet for a spell until we get ready to burn gunpowder. Once we get ready for action, though — well, I expect everything will burst wide open when that time comes."

"And I hope it isn't far off."

"I've got a feeling in my bones it isn't, Caliper. Keep your gun in a loose holster. Mark my words, trouble is coming!"

10. A Council of War

Just why Straub Krouch had ordered his men to meet in the bunkhouse that afternoon, none of the punchers were certain. Plainly something important was afoot. The men arrived in twos and threes at the appointed hour. Among them were two strangers who had arrived at the Circle-Slash that morning. They had the appearance of gun fighters — which they were. Neither of the two had had a great deal to say, keeping to themselves and refusing to mix with the other Circle-Slash hands. About all the regular cowpunchers had learned regarding them were their names: one was called the Nevada Kid; the other was named Trigger Ronson.

The Nevada Kid was a swarthy-faced, beady-eyed slim man with a wisp of black mustache, a quiet manner and a somewhat dandified appearance. He wore a canary-yellow shirt and much cheap jewelry. There was a beaded throat-latch attached to his fawn-colored sombrero. Trigger Ronson was tall and muscular with pale blue eyes and a restless manner. Killer was written all over him. The holstered Colt's .45s at the hips of these two looked extremely efficient.

Straub Krouch sat at the desk of his fore-man, Ward Austen. Austen was a rather slov-enly looking man with muddy-colored hair and weak eyes. His overalls were dirty, and he didn't look as though he'd shaved for two weeks. Next to Austen stood Hedge Furlow, Austen's right-hand man. Furlow was a coward at heart and looked it. Next to Furlow was Cal Webster, a blustering, bully-ing man who had recently come to work for the Circle-Slash. Stan Cox, his broken arms bandaged and in slings, sat on an upturned empty box. There were a half a dozen other Circle-Slash punchers there — all hard-bitten men who were thoroughly familiar with Krouch's methods and approved of them.

The bunkhouse was thick with swirling cig-arette smoke. Some of the men chewed to-bacco. No one said a great deal. They were all waiting to learn the reason for Krouch bringing them together. Krouch sat moodily at his foreman's desk, a long black cigar jut-ting at an angle from his thick lips.

Finally Krouch opened the conversation, after clearing his throat. "I suppose all you hombres are wondering what I had you meet here for. Well, one or two things have come up, and I figure it's best that you all know the lay of the land, before we go any farther. In the first place, you cowpokes that have been in the habit of going into Orejano and raising merry hell — and especially on pay-days —

are going to have to tone down a mite."

Ward Austen looked a trifle startled. "If I'd known, chief, that you wanted the boys kept on a tight rein," he said ingratiatingly, "I'd have bopped down on 'em long ago. But I never did figure that —"

"Don't get me wrong, Ward," Krouch interrupted. "S'far as I'm concerned the boys can get drunk and shoot up the town all they like so long as they do their work when they're needed. But I'm not the one who's complainin'. Some of the so-called better citizens of the town" — Krouch sneered nastily — "have been kicking to the county authorities. The result is I've just learned that the sheriff has been asked to appoint a deputy, with office in Orejano. I stalled that off as long as possible, but that's the situation —"

"When's the deputy comin'?" a puncher asked. "Maybe we can make things hot for him, so he won't stay."

"None of that, Burley," Krouch shook his head. "We've just got to act peaceful — when we're in town — for a spell. Eventually I'll get squared around, and in time we'll have things back like they was before. You all hear me — tone down! I don't want to have to tell you again. And I don't know just when the damn deputy is due to arrive."

"Mebbe we all better start going to church," a cowhand guffawed. Somebody said something about robbing the collection plate, and the room rocked with laughter. Finally the noise subsided. Krouch went on, "I didn't bring you all here just for that, of course. We got more serious business to talk over, something that concerns every man here. The fact is last night, or early this morning, rather, somebody spied on our ghost herd. You that were there when it happened know all about it, but I'm telling the rest of you so you'll know what's what."

A chorus of voices broke out, some consternation was shown. Cal Webster said, "How do you know you were spied on?"

Krouch replied grimly, "Because somebody took a shot at the rider — damn nigh got him, too."

That brought more excited questions.

Cal Webster said, "Aw, there's no use getting too excited. It was probably some Mex happened to be cutting across the range that done the spying. Maybe he got nervous and his gun went off by accident."

Ward Austen snorted, "That's what you think, Cal, but you're a heap mistaken. There's no Mex around here can shoot that good, by accident or otherwise. That was intentional. If it had been your turn to be the rider last night you'd understand I'm talking straight. That bullet passed so close to my nose I could smell the heat. I just wish it had been your turn to be Constado's ghost last night."

Webster grinned scornfully. "What did you do about it?"

Austen said a bit sheepishly, "I high-tailed it for cover as quick as possible — same's you'd done in my boots. Later me and a couple of the boys got our horses and looked over the country some. We figured the shot had come from the big hogback over that way. Come daylight we climbed the hogback and, sure enough, there was a sign where somebody had been watchin' us."

"Who was it?" a puncher asked.

Krouch growled. "If we knew there wouldn't be no need for this meeting. I'd seen to it that our troubles were squared away by this time. Go on, Ward."

Ward Austen continued, "We don't know who it was, but there was the sign of two men there. Judging from what tracks we could read, they left plumb sudden after throwing that lead slug in my direction —"

"They left sudden, eh?" Trigger Ronson put in. "That sounds like a couple of greasers that got scared off. White men wouldn't run —"

"Some wouldn't," Krouch agreed, "but a couple of smart hombres would know enough to high tail it before they were captured by a gang. That's what I'm afraid of, that we're up against somebody that's damn nigh as smart as we are."

"Maybe it was Tanner and one of his

men," Stan Cox put in.

Krouch shook his head. "I thought of that. But I know Tanner. If it had been Tanner, the talk would have been around town by this time. I was in town at noontime. I didn't hear of anything unusual. Tanner would be all for raising a gang to get to the bottom of the ghost business, and we'd hear of it. It wasn't Tanner. Nope, whoever it was is keeping his mouth shut until he can learn more. He's smart. I don't like it."

"But who could it be?" Cal Webster wanted to know.

"That's what brings us to the reason for this meeting," Krouch said. "I'm thinking about those two cow-willies who hit Orejano yesterday, Nogales Scott and Caliper Maxwell."

He smiled grimly. "Hedge and Stan encountered 'em at the Apache yesterday."

Stan Cox and Hedge Furlow burst into a fit of cursing.

Krouch told them to shut up and continued, "I've a hunch it might be them two. If so, they'd be bad medicine for us. We know they can shoot. They're strangers here. I don't like the idea of 'em staying at the Star-M. No telling what they got in mind. They might even be range detectives sent here by the cattle association. Yesterday I was all for hiring 'em on my pay roll. Now I've changed my mind since that shot last night.

They're friends of Tanner, too. Course Tanner just met them yesterday, but we've only got his word for that; to cut this story short I'd feel better if Scott and Maxwell weren't around here a-tall. They're just the sort that might get snoopy and mess up our game."

"What's the answer?" Hedge Furlow wanted to know.

"They've got to be rubbed out," Krouch said bluntly, "and the job has got to be done before that deputy gets appointed in Orejano. After we get rid of Scott and Maxwell we can get peaceful, but not until then."

"Who's going to do the job?" Furlow asked.

"You're going to help," Krouch said.

Furlow paled. "Well, now, look here, boss —" he commenced.

"Don't stall, Hedge," Krouch grunted. "You —"

Cal Webster interrupted. "Ain't showing yellow, are you, Hedge? Did you get too much of that pair's gunwork yesterday?"

Stan Cox sneered. "He didn't get any of it. He didn't stay long enough."

"Well," Furlow said lamely, "I wouldn't have run out on you, Stan, if I'd knowed you wasn't right behind me. I didn't realize there was just those two. I thought there must have been a half-dozen or so —"

"Bushwah!" Cal Webster snorted. "You lost

your nerve, Hedge. It's too bad I wasn't there to back Stan's play. I'd have showed them two cow-nurses what shootin' really is —"

"I'll give you that chance, Cal," Krouch said coldly. "You've talked a lot. I'll give you a chance to see what you can do to back up that big talk."

Webster gulped, then nodded. "All right," he blustered. "I'll take it."

"So it's up to you and Hedge then," Krouch stated.

Hedge Furlow didn't look very happy about the situation. Webster said, "Fact is, boss, I'd just as soon have somebody else instead of Hedge. He's backed down from that pair once. How do I know he won't do it again?"

Krouch said, "Because I'm giving you two insurance on the job of wiping out Maxwell and Scott."

Furlow said, "Insurance? In what way?"

Krouch motioned toward the Nevada Kid and Trigger Ronson. "I brought Ronson and the Kid here to do a little work on Lee Tanner. Right now we can let Tanner go for a spell. So the Kid and Ronson can back any play that you and Cal make when you meet Scott and Maxwell. That gives you odds of two to one. It shouldn't be any trouble wiping out those two hombres. In fact, you've got everything on your side."

Furlow and Webster looked brighter at the prospect. Through the minds of both ran the thought that they'd let Trigger Ronson and the Nevada Kid carry the burden of the work.

Trigger Ronson said restlessly, "Looka here, Krouch. You imported me and the Kid to do a certain job on a man named Tanner. The price was all set and agreed to. Now don't you get any idea that you're going to get two jobs for the price of one — or maybe you could call it three jobs. Me'n the Kid don't do business on those terms."

"Don't you worry, Ronson," Krouch snapped irritatedly. "I expect to pay you — and pay you well — for *each* job you do. There'll be extra cash for Maxwell and Scott."

"That's all we're interested in — cash money." The Nevada Kid smiled silkily. "At so much a head the job looks like a cinch, eh, Trigger?"

"I'm satisfied." Trigger Ronson nodded. "Just how do you want the job done, Krouch?"

"Satisfactorily," Krouch snapped. "Pick a scrap with them two and let 'em have it. Hell's bells! The planning is up to you. That's what I'm paying for. You and the Kid and Furlow and Webster get together. Work it out your own way. Just make sure that my name doesn't appear in it in any way. And don't forget, Kid — Ronson — nobody knows you're on my pay roll. I don't want anybody to learn it, either. But get the job done and get it done right. I won't rest easy about our game until Maxwell and Scott are blasted out of existence. Blast 'em, see, blast 'em!"

11. War Talk

For a couple of days Caliper and Nogales stayed close to the Star-M. Neither would have admitted, had they been asked, that they were enjoying working in the vicinity of their lady boss but each was hard hit — or at least thought he was. They spent their time working about the ranch buildings, getting old equipment in shape, mending harnesses, painting the stables and in general getting affairs shipshape on the Star-M.

They had dropped down on the bench in the shade of the bunkhouse one afternoon just after dinner. Old Pablo was puttering about the place somewhere, and Lena Lou was inside working about the house. They could hear the girl's voice raised in an old lullaby while she swept, or dusted or washed the dishes. Whatever it was she was doing they weren't certain.

Nogales inhaled deeply on his cigarette and ground the butt in the earth under one heel. "I've been thinking —" he commenced.

"I knew there was something the matter with you," Caliper cut in, "you've been complaining of having a headache so often."

"That's something you've never had, anyway," Nogales said sweetly. "You have to have something in a head to make it ache. Your skull's so empty I can hear an echo every time you grunt."

Caliper winced, grinned then, at a loss for a retort, decided to talk sense until he could think of something to needle his pardner. "All right, all right," he said good-naturedly, "I'll admit you drew blood that time. What's on your mind?"

Nogales smiled slowly and commenced, "It's this way. I've been thinking that it's a shame that Lena Lou has been robbed of her cattle and now stands to lose her ranch unless something is done about it. You know, she's a dang nice girl — not a girl you'd be interested in of course, but for some decent, hard-working puncher —"

"What makes you think I wouldn't be interested in her?" Caliper demanded.

"Oh, she wants somebody more her style. Somebody that understands women. Naturally she wouldn't go for any hard-drinking, gambling galoot like you. She'd want a man who was settled down and peaceful to help her run her outfit. You can understand what I mean —"

"We-ell, yes." Caliper frowned. "But, shucks, Nogales, I'm not what you'd call a hard-drinking man. I don't drink near the amount you do."

Nogales shrugged his shoulders. "Me, I can

take it or leave it. Never did care for the stuff. I just drink to be sociable. Fact of the matter is, I've been thinking lately of going on the water wagon. It's just plain foolishness to spend your money for liquor when you come to think of it."

"I've been thinking of doing the same thing," Caliper said. "I was figuring out just last night all the money I've tossed across bars in my time. It's plumb shameful, that's a fact. I said to myself, 'Caliper, you should swear off. You're just not doing yourself any good.' So I decided then and there never to touch another drop."

"Well, now, Caliper," Nogales advised, "you don't want to do anything hasty. Why don't you let me try it for a spell and find out how it goes? You wouldn't want to swear off and then, if the going got too tough, break your pledge. No decent woman — er — er — nobody wants anything to do with a man who can't keep his word, even if it's only to himself."

"That's right too. It's pretty hard, once you quit a thing, Nogales, not to touch it again. I already quit gambling, like I told you I was —"

"You did?" Nogales looked startled. "When did this happen?"

"Just yesterday I made up my mind. It was while you were painting the barn and I was rawhiding those corral poles. Lena Lou come up and she was talking to me —"

"About what?" Nogales said quickly.

"Oh, one thing and another," Caliper said airily. "I don't remember exactly what was said. We were sort of talking about life being a gamble and that couples who got married never were sure if — anyway, I got to talking about gambling and I told her how I'd sworn off and hadn't touched a card since the last time I played and so on, like that. It was all quiet, dignified talk like Lena Lou would like. You wouldn't have cared about it even if you'd understood. I told her how I didn't care much about high society and that all I cared for, when I got ready to settle down, was just a plain little home and no fancy cooking —"

Nogales was making choking sounds and finally managed to ask, "And what did Lena Lou say to all that?"

"She allowed I sounded right sensible and said she admired a man with such ideas."

"Not meaning you, of course."

"Well," Caliper said modestly, "she didn't mention any names, of course, but I could guess what way the wind blew."

"Uh-huh," Nogales said absent-mindedly. "I wonder if there's a church in Orejano."

"What kind of a church — Baptist, Methodist — ?"

"It don't make any difference what kind."

"Nogales! Don't tell me you're thinking of

joining the church?"

"Why not?" Nogales asked doggedly. "A feller gets tired of brawling around after a while when he gets ready to settle down. You'll notice women always like a man that goes reg'lar to church and is one of the pillars of the — er — place —"

"Pillar?" Caliper frowned. "I thought a pillar was something to hold up a porch roof — or a temple — or something. Wasn't there a feller called Samson, in the Bible, that knocked down all the pillars in the temple?"

"There maybe was. But don't mention that name to me. All I can think of is Tuck Samson. And his half brother, Straub Krouch, I don't like any better. Say, you didn't say anything to Lena Lou about us seeing the ghost herd, did you?"

Caliper shook his head. "I've been thinking about those ghosts a lot, too."

"You and me both. I've got a notion to ride into Orejano. . . ."

"To see if there's a church there?"

"No. I'd just like to sort of circulate around and see if there's any talk about that ghost herd. I might hear something interesting."

"It's not a bad idea. Let's go."

"I'd just as soon stay here, Caliper, if you want to run in alone."

"What are you aiming to do?" Caliper asked suspiciously.

"Nothing. Why?" Nogales asked innocently.

"Well, it was your idea, that's all. Don't you back up your own ideas?"

"Ever know me not to?" Nogales said grouchily. "All right, let's get our ponies. We might learn something new."

Five minutes later they were mounted and pounding along the trail that led to Orejano.

It was close to three in the afternoon when they rode into the town. Their throats were parched and dry from the dusty trail and they headed at once toward Johnnie Armstrong's Bluebonnet Bar, after dropping their ponies' reins over the hitch rail.

"See anything of Straub Krouch or his scum?" Nogales said.

Caliper shook his head. "If they're in town they're probably in the Apache Saloon."

Several horses were tethered along the street. The Apache Saloon's tie rail was full. There weren't many pedestrians on the sidewalks. A few Mexicans dozed in the shade between buildings. Caliper and Nogales walked on toward the entrance to the Bluebonnet.

They passed through the swinging doors and spoke to Johnnie Armstrong standing behind the bar. There weren't any customers in the place. Johnnie's face lighted up when he saw them. "H'are you, Nogales — Caliper?"

They told him the present state of their

health, then Nogales said, "Got any more of that cold beer?"

"Plenty."

"I'll want one bottle, anyway."

"Trot 'er out, Johnnie," Caliper nodded. He turned suddenly. "Hey, Nogales, I thought you were going to swear off drinking."

Nogales said apologetically, "We-ell, you see, Caliper, I'm just sort of tapering off. It's not good for a man to swear off too sudden. Besides, I've got to wash the dust from my throat. It's pretty dangerous —"

"Dust is?" Caliper asked blankly.

"Very dangerous," Nogales said emphatically, warming to his subject. "There's thousands of germs in dust, and I might get a bad throat ailment if I didn't wash it out. So you see, this beer" — pouring a full glass of the foamy amber — "isn't really a drink I'm taking. I sort of look on it as a preventative medicine — something that's necessary to my health."

"Oh, I see," Caliper said dryly.

Johnnie busied himself, putting more beer to cool. After a few minutes Nogales said, "With beer like that on hand, Johnnie, I don't see why you don't have more customers."

"I should have, but —" Johnnie hesitated.

"But what?" Caliper asked.

Johnnie said meaningly, "There's a right ornery gang hangs out at the Apache."

"You mean," Nogales frowned, "that they intimidate your customers?"

"They make it uncomfortable for any of my customers seen coming in here," Johnnie explained.

"Must be," Caliper said, "that nobody saw us coming in here."

Johnnie said, "I've been wondering about that."

"I should think," Nogales advanced, "that after the way we shot up the Apache three days ago there wouldn't be much business there."

"Oh, they got the Apache to running again that same night," Johnnie Armstrong explained, "after Mike Artora had done a bit of reddin' up. Mike salvaged quite a bit of his stock and borrowed or begged the rest from the two saloons down the street."

"Did you let him have any stuff?" Caliper asked.

"Some — at the regular retail price. That's why I'm not so popular with Artora and the gang that hangs out there. I understand Straub Krouch has put in an order for a new mirror too. He plans to fix the Apache all up." Johnnie hesitated a moment then continued, "Hedge Furlow — he's the hombre that jumped on his horse and beat a retreat that day you hombres put on your gun party — has been hanging around the last day or so, doing a heap of talking about what he'd do to you two if he ever met you again."

Nogales laughed. "Furlow must have got his nerve back. Is he going to take us both on at once?"

"He's got a pal with him that's backing up his war talk," Johnnie explained. "Circle-Slash puncher named Cal Webster — loud-mouthed galoot but pretty good hand with a gun. Then there's a couple of strangers in town, mean-looking coyotes named Trigger Ronson and the Nevada Kid. They look like hired gun fighters to me. They've been hanging around the Apache a lot, not saying much, though."

"Are they Circle-Slash hands?" Nogales asked.

"Not that I know of," Johnnie replied. "They don't mingle much with anybody. I've seen 'em talking to Webster and Furlow once or twice." He shook his head. "I can't say I like the type of men who're coming to Orejano. Instead of getting better the town is getting worse."

"What's needed here," Nogales said soberly, "is a law-and-order officer. Somebody should insist that the county sheriff maintain a deputy here all the time — instead of just sending one here to open his office a few days a month, like I understand has been done —"

"That's one advance the town has made," Johnnie cut in. "Some of the better people

139

here got together and wrote to the county authorities. There'll be a deputy appointed right soon, with a permanent office here."

"That's a step in the right direction, anyway," Caliper nodded.

"Who's due to be appointed?" Nogales asked.

Before he had time to finish the question or receive a reply from Johnnie Armstrong, Hedge Furlow pushed through the swinging doors, followed by Cal Webster. At sight of the two cowboys at the bar Furlow said something in an undertone to Webster. Webster scowled, and the two men continued on toward the bar.

"What'll it be, gents?" Johnnie inquired with cold courtesy.

"Beer," Webster said. "Lots of it."

"Three or four cases, anyway," Furlow added.

"Cases?" Johnnie looked puzzled.

Webster explained, "Artora needs beer over to his place. Bring a couple of cases over there *pronto,* Armstrong. He'll pay you when it arrives."

Johnnie shook his head. "Artora can't have any more of my stock, men. If you want to drink here, I'll be glad to serve you."

"You'll bring it across the street, like we tell you," Webster blustered bullyingly. Again Johnnie shook his head.

"We don't care to drink here at all," Furlow put in.

140

Nogales' soft laughter broke in on the conversation. "You'd better make up your mind, Furlow," he advised, "to drink here — or hereafter."

Webster and Furlow looked angrily at the two cowboys. Furlow said, "You'd better keep out of this, cowpoke. It's none of your business."

Caliper said, "Last time we cut in on your business, Furlow, you ran like a scared jack rabbit. You'd better repeat before you get hurt."

"Who in hell you talking to?" Webster bellowed.

"We-ell —" Caliper hesitated then glanced gravely at Nogales. "Pard, what would you say I was talking to? He looks like a windbag to me, but I wouldn't be sure."

"By Gawd," Webster rasped, "I believe you two are looking for trouble!"

"Not looking for it," Nogales said gently, shaking his head. "We're forcing it on you. It's taken a long time for the idea to penetrate your thick skulls."

Webster tensed. "Me and my pard will accommodate you, any time, anywhere —"

Johnnie Armstrong came up from behind the bar, a sawed-off shotgun cradled under one arm. "Don't any man reach for an iron!" he warned, swinging the double muzzle in a short arc to cover the men in front of the bar. "You, Webster — Furlow — if this is a scheme to shoot up my Bluebonnet it don't work. If there's any lead slinging done it will be done outside my door. Now you'd better get out."

Webster nodded angrily. "All right, Armstrong. We'll get out but we'll settle with you later. First we got a score to settle with these two cow-nurses who seem to be hunting trouble." He swung on Caliper and Nogales. "You two game to shoot it out with us outside?"

"Not only game but anxious," Nogales snapped. "We'll meet you out on the street in five minutes."

"Wait a minute," Furlow put in, "I don't like this idea of shooting on Main Street. Some innocent folks — women and kids — might get hit by stray bullets. Suppose we meet at the Tip-Top Corral? You cow-nurses know where the Tip-Top is?"

"We can find it," Caliper said coldly. "Get going. We'll meet you there. And you'd better have your guns smoking when we arrive. It'll be too late afterward!"

Webster snarled. "You'll probably fork your bronc and fan the wind the minute we leave but if you're game, we'll meet you two at the Tip-Top in fifteen minutes. C'mon, Hedge."

He and Furlow started for the door. Nogales called after them, "That fanning the wind works two ways. We'll be surprised if we find you there — alone. Now get out of here, or I won't be able to hold my lead. I'm getting plumb impatient to drill a couple of snakes."

Webster swore and started to turn back. The gun in Armstrong's hands lifted. "You heard your orders, Webster, you'd better get going before this scatter-gun beats you to the start."

"C'mon, Cal," Furlow said nervously, pushing past his pardner in his hurry to gain the street. "We'll do our arguing with hot lead."

"You may argue," Caliper called after them, "but aces to tens we have the last word!"

This time there was no reply from the two men.

12. Tip-Top Gunplay!

The swinging doors of the Bluebonnet finally ceased all movement. No one had said anything for a moment. Then Nogales drawled, "That's always the way. I try my best to be peaceful, but Caliper's hot temper has got us into trouble again. And I'll have to back his play."

Caliper chuckled, "I'd like to see anybody keep *you* out of trouble, you long-legged son of a gun!"

The remarks weren't funny to Johnnie Armstrong. He was serious faced, a trifle pale. He heaved a long sigh and replaced his shotgun under the bar. "Maybe I should have pulled triggers when I had 'em covered," he said reluctantly.

Nogales shook his head. "It would have been murder. Those two had no intention of drawing irons in here. For some reason they want to fight it out some place else."

"The reason probably being," Caliper said, "that they expect to meet us with reinforcements. They were figuring on picking a fight with us when they came in but they kept their hands well away from their guns, so we wouldn't start action too soon. Johnnie, was that Cal Webster with Furlow?"

Armstrong nodded. "That was Webster. He's pretty fast on the draw."

Nogales nodded. "Webster's nerve is all right, but Furlow didn't look none too anxious for a meeting. I figure he's got something up his sleeve that bolstered up his nerve."

Johnnie said, "I wonder." Stooping below his bar, he came up with a beer case filled with bottles, on one end of which was stamped the name of the maker, Eagle Brewing Company. Hoisting the case to his shoulder, he started around the end of the bar.

Caliper said, "Where you going?"

Without turning, Johnnie replied, "Artora sent word I was to bring over a few cases. I'd better get busy."

"Hey, Johnnie," Caliper spoke sharply. "You going to do as Artora and those two skunks ordered? Looks to me like you'd lost your nerve."

"It looks that way," Johnnie admitted as he pushed his way through the swinging doors and out to the street.

Caliper looked blankly at Nogales. "Well, I'll be damned!" he exploded suddenly.

"You probably will," Nogales nodded placidly, "if you jump to conclusions too soon. Wait."

Within a few minutes Johnnie returned

minus the case. He took up his position behind the bar and said quietly, "There's the usual crowd in the Apache with four exceptions. Artora mentioned that Cal Webster and Hedge Furlow have started for the Tip-Top Corral. The rest of the customers are getting ready to head down there now and watch the fight."

"You mentioned *four* exceptions," Nogales pointed out.

Johnnie nodded. "The other two who aren't there are the Nevada Kid and Trigger Ronson."

"That means, Caliper," Nogales said thoughtfully, "that we'll be facing four men instead of just Webster and Furlow. They figure to hold a surprise party for us. Thanks to Johnnie carrying that beer across the street we've been warned."

"Gosh, Johnnie" — Caliper was covered with apologetic confusion — "I'm sorry. I thought you'd lost your nerve."

Johnnie smiled wanly. "I damn near did but I suspected some skulduggery. You two deserve a square break. I wanted to find out what I could."

Nogales said, "Probably Artora didn't pay you for that beer. I'll take care of it." He produced some bills from his pocket.

Johnnie shook his head. "Don't worry. That was a case of empties. Artora was so busy ordering me just where to put it down that he didn't notice the bottles were empty. But forget me and Artora. What are you two going to do? You can't take on such odds as four against two."

Nogales said, "We've taken on worse and we're still alive."

Caliper said, "Where is this Tip-Top Corral?"

Johnnie explained how to find it: "It's on this side of the street, heading east. Let me see. . . . It's just the other side of the general store. That's eight — no, nine doors from here. The Tip-Top Corral is just a vacant lot between the general store and another building. The other building is a big barn, empty at present. The corral is oblong shaped. It's fenced in at the front where you'll enter a gate that usually stands open. The back end is fenced across, but there's no gate there —"

"What kind of a fence?" Nogales asked.

"Three-pole wooden fence," Johnnie replied. "The top pole is about head high. The corral isn't used much. The feller that owns the barn, which makes one side of the corral, had an idea of holding horse auctions there at one time, but nobody was interested, seems like. Like I say, it's just an oblong enclosure, with buildings forming two sides and fences at the front and back."

Caliper said, "We'd better get started, pard."

Nogales said, "Wait a minute. We've got to do some planning. Remember we're outnumbered four to two. That requires a mite of thought." He pondered a minute. "There'll be four guns there watching the street, waiting for us to appear. The instant we show up they'll tear loose with their cutters. Suppose only one of us showed up. They'd be surprised. They might not shoot at once —"

"I'll be the one to go," Caliper put in.

"Shut up, I'm trying to think —"

"I know it's an effort, Nogales, but —"

"I told you to shut up. . . . Look, Johnnie, if Caliper left by your back door and walked east he'd arrive at the back fence of the corral, wouldn't he?"

Johnnie nodded. "He couldn't miss it. But there's no gate to enter by in the back. There's just a gate on the street side."

Nogales said, "I understand. I reckon I better go the back way. My legs are longer than Caliper's and I can get over the fence faster. Caliper takes the street route. We both arrive at the same time."

Caliper was getting the idea now. He drew his gun, spun the cylinder and replaced the weapon in holster. "Let's go," he said tersely. "Good luck, pard. See you later, Johnnie."

"By Gawd, he takes it cool," Johnnie gasped, gazing after Caliper's retreating form as it passed through the swinging doors.

"Nogales, I'd sure never dream he was headed for a fight."

There wasn't any answer. A door slammed at the rear of the saloon, and Johnnie turned to find that Nogales had departed at the same instant as Caliper. "What a pair, what a pair!" Johnnie muttered. "God help 'em now, though. They're up against too much." His thoughts turned upon his own troubles. "Once Caliper and Nogales are taken care of, those scuts will come here to raise hell with me. Reckon I'd better get prepared." He stooped below the bar and brought his shotgun back into sight, laid it on the bar and placed a box of shells within easy reaching distance.

Then he waited, tense, listening, every nerve a-quiver. The minutes dragged. It seemed an hour passed — though it wasn't more than five or six minutes — when he heard a sudden burst of gunfire from the direction of the Tip-Top Corral. . . .

After leaving the Bluebonnet Saloon, Caliper stepped into the street and headed east along the sidewalk in the direction of the Tip-Top Corral, adapting his gait to a speed that he knew Nogales would employ, thus bringing both men to the scene of action at the same time. There were several people along the street now. No one spoke to Caliper, though he was watched with curious eyes. News of the fight had spread around town.

Caliper heard one man say, "He's alone. His pardner has backed out. They ain't got *that* waddie's nerve, though. He'll be wiped out. . . ."

Similar whispered comments were heard as Caliper strode on, eyes straight ahead. Men fell in behind and followed at a respectful distance. Across the street from the gateway of the Tip-Top Corral a group of hard citizens from the Apache Saloon had gathered to watch the slaughter, as they termed it. Suddenly a shout went up from this group, "He's coming alone! Maxwell's alone. Scott ain't with him! Scott's fanned tail outta these parts!"

The excited cries increased as Caliper drew near the corral. He passed the Orejano Saddle Store where a man stood peering out of a doorway. "Good luck, feller," the man whispered hoarsely.

One by one buildings passed to his rear. Ahead, just beyond the Paris Barber Shop, was the general store. He passed the barber shop and the general store. He could see the bars of the pole corral now, with the long gate standing wide open, looking like an invitation to a death trap.

Caliper headed for the open gateway, hands swinging at his sides. He didn't break stride as he stepped through the opening. Ten paces inside the opening Hedge Furlow, the Nevada Kid, Cal Webster and Trigger

Ronson were standing, spread out, their hands tense above holsters.

At sight of Caliper, alone, they paused in surprise.

Webster snarled, "Did that yellow pard of yours lose his nerve?"

Hedge Furlow yelled excitedly, "Kill Maxwell, anyway. We got him —"

And then, from back of the gunmen, came Nogales' cool voice: "I'm ready any time you are, pard."

There had been warning cries from across the street as Nogales leaped to the top pole of the corral fence, but none of the gunmen had heard them, so intent were they on watching Caliper. Now, at sound of Nogales' voice, Furlow, Trigger Ronson and Cal Webster whirled, in sudden confusion, to face the voice. Only the Nevada Kid retained the presence of mind not to turn. Instead, his hands dipped to the guns at his sides. Fast as he was, Caliper's draw was an instant swifter. White fire flashed from his right hand, even as the Nevada Kid's guns were leaving holsters.

The three men who had swung about at sound of Nogales' voice now turned back in some confusion to face Caliper, half expecting that Caliper was already drawing on them. Realizing they had been outwitted, Trigger Ronson and Cal Webster again swerved toward Nogales, just leaping into the corral from the top of the fence.

Even while he was in the air Nogales was thumbing hot lead from his six-shooter. He was moving too fast to make an accurate mark for the guns of Webster and Ronson. The Nevada Kid was down now but still firing one gun. Caliper had whirled and tossed a quick shot at Hedge Furlow which missed aim.

Trigger Ronson had dropped before Nogales' first bullet. Webster fired at Nogales, crouched down and fired a second time. Nogales threw another shot at Webster. Webster screamed and crumpled to one side. The guns were roaring like mad now.

Hedge Furlow was shooting wildly at Caliper, missing all his shots. Suddenly he flung his gun to the earth and fled frantically toward the rear fence. Nogales was closing in fast toward the center of the corral. He flung one quick sidewise shot at Furlow as Furlow passed him. Without pausing to see the effect of his bullet, Nogales unleashed another stream of lead and smoke in the direction of the Nevada Kid who, while prone on the earth, was just drawing a bead on Caliper.

Caliper threw one shot at Webster and another at Furlow, who was just plunging to earth from the effect of Nogales' fire. That seemed to end matters. The roaring of the guns was silenced. Powder smoke drifted thickly in the warm air, then vanished in tiny swirls as the breeze lifted it beyond the corral.

Four men were down in the corral dust. Trigger Ronson and the Nevada Kid lay silent, though the Kid's body still quivered now and then. Cal Webster was fighting to rise again, but the gun had fallen from his grasp and he was no longer dangerous. Hedge Furlow was moaning with pain between his cries of surrender, and crawling toward the rear fence on all fours.

A sudden shout had gone up from the Apache crowd standing across the street. A moment the crowd hesitated, then started toward the corral, angry voices filling the air.

"Keep 'em covered, pard," Nogales yelled. "My gun's empty. I've got to reload!"

While Nogales was shoving in fresh cartridges, Caliper swung his gun toward the approaching crowd, swinging the gun in a wide arc that seemed to cover every man.

"Keep back, you scuts!" Caliper yelled. "I'll drill the first hombre that comes a step nearer. And don't reach for guns. You may get me, but I'll get you first."

The crowd came to a sudden stop and commenced to back away. A number of men threw their arms in the air. By this time Nogales had his gun loaded. His eyes blazed angrily. "Now, if you scourin's want trouble, we're ready for you. We've downed your sidewinder pals and we're ready to take you on any time."

Caliper laughed. "They didn't know I was bluffin' 'em, Nogales. Now you keep 'em covered while I reload. My gun was empty, too."

He was replenishing his cylinder, while the crowd continued to back away before Nogales' threatening six-shooter. Nogales tilted his weapon threateningly, speaking to the retreating crowd: "You hombres better get back to the Apache before I decide to let daylight through a few of you — but, wait! you with the yellow shirt; you, tall feller with the mustache" — singling out certain men from the crowd — "and you with them striped pants — you three fellers come into this corral and check up on these would-be gun fighters. See if they're dead, or who can be taken to a doctor. The rest of you, beat it, and beat it *pronto!*"

By this time Caliper had his six-shooter loaded and was covering the crowd with Nogales. The three men indicated stepped reluctantly forward and entered the corral. The rest of the crowd commenced to scatter, then moved hastily off down the street in the direction of the Apache Saloon.

Nogales spoke to the three men he had called across the street: "Get busy, hombres, check the casualties."

While he and Caliper watched the street, ready for any more signs of hostility which might develop, the three men went among the prone gunmen. In a few minutes the tall man with the mustache reported to Nogales and Caliper: "Both the Nevada Kid and Trigger Ronson are dead. I don't figure Cal Webster will live more'n a few hours. He's unconscious now. Hedge Furlow ain't hurt much. Got some skin furrowed off one leg, lost more skin off'n his ribs, and one knuckle on his right hand is nicked. He was just crawling over the fence when I got to him. I told him he'd better wait."

Nogales laughed shortly. "Caliper, it looks like we'd made a cleanup."

"I reckon, pard. Maybe this will be a warning to any more scuts that are looking for trouble —"

The tall man with the mustache broke in admiringly, "It shore oughter be a warning to some folks. I ain't never seen no lead slingin' like you two hombres staged. I'm shore pleased to make the acquaintance of you two gents —"

"Cut it," Nogales snapped contemptuously. "You had plenty chance to make our acquaintance before, feller. Salve don't go now. You and your two pals take care of them dead bodies. If anything can be done for Webster, do it. Tell Hedge Furlow to get on his bronc and fan his tail out of this section. If I ever see him again I'll blast him wide open. And from now on you hombres from the Apache better walk plumb cautious.

Don't cross our trails any more than you can help."

"Yes sir," the man said humbly, glancing over his shoulder at his two companions who were bending over Cal Webster, "but I don't want you should get us wrong; we didn't have nothing to do with this."

"Except," Caliper snapped, "you stood across the street waiting to see us slaughtered, outnumbered by some professional gunmen. Phaugh! You coyotes make me sick."

"Yes sir," the man said again, his manner meek. "I'm sure regretful that —"

"Aw, shucks, Caliper," Nogales growled contemptuously, "come on, let's get out of here. These hombres can take care of their friends."

The two cowboys departed from the corral and started back toward the Bluebonnet Bar. When halfway there they met Straub Krouch who was hurrying along the sidewalk, his features set in a black frown. As his gaze fell on the two cowboys he slowed pace.

"Keep right on going, Krouch," Nogales said. "Follow your nose and you'll find your men — though maybe not the way you expected to find them."

"I don't know what you're talking about," Krouch said nervously. "I just heard that two of my men had had a fight with you, but —"

"Four of your men," Caliper corrected.

Krouch shook his head. "I don't know anything about those other two, haven't the least idea how all this happened. I just got through telling my hands a couple of days ago that I didn't want any more rowdyism in Orejano. If they picked a fight, it's their own fault. Good riddance to 'em, I say."

"Hedge Furlow is the only one left," Nogales said. "I warned him to get out of this country."

"That saves me the trouble of telling him the same thing," Krouch growled. "I hope you two boys won't hold me responsible for this trouble."

Caliper shook his head. "It's never any trouble for us, Krouch, to wipe out a nest of sidewinders."

"By cripes!" Krouch said, "I believe you two do think I had something to do with the fight."

"Oh my, no," Nogales said sweetly. "We know you're too peace loving for that, Mister Krouch. We wouldn't think of blaming you — much! Come on, Caliper."

They passed on, leaving the scowling Krouch staring after them on the sidewalk. Krouch finally turned away, cursing, and continued on toward the corral.

Caliper and Nogales walked along the street until they came to the Bluebonnet Bar. They entered and found the bar lined with customers, many of whom were regular clients of the Apache Saloon.

Johnnie stretched his gaze above the heads of the crowd. "Congrats," he grinned. "Have a drink on the house."

Nogales said, "Looks like business has increased in our absence."

Johnnie nodded. "I've been right busy the last ten minutes."

Caliper said, "I reckon a heap of folks are learning they don't have to drink at the Apache if they don't want to. I figure there's a new setup in Orejano."

A man at the bar turned around, saying, "I hope it keeps that way. There's been a bad element here running things to suit themselves."

"And we figure that's just about finished, too." Nogales nodded. "Caliper and I have made our start. With the help of the decent punchers in this neck of the range we aim to see things through to a finish. And that's a direct warning for anybody who isn't in favor of law and order. Set 'em up, Johnnie. We're ready for that drink now."

13. Good Strategy

It was shortly after supper had commenced that Nogales and Caliper arrived back at the Star-M. Lee Tanner had called that afternoon and had been prevailed upon by Lena Lou to stay for the meal. The girl, old Pablo and Tanner were seated at the table when the two cowboys came in.

"We waited for you boys," Lena Lou said, "and then finally decided not to wait longer. But you're in time; draw up chairs."

"You don't want ever to wait for Nogales," Caliper chuckled. "There's no telling when he'll ever show up."

They drew up chairs, and Lena Lou placed steaming plates of food before them. For a time no one spoke; everyone was busily engaged in consuming food.

Lee Tanner asked, between mouthfuls of juicy steak, "You boys been in Orejano all afternoon?"

Caliper nodded and went on eating. Nogales said, "Didn't get around to leaving until after five o'clock. We were talking to some fellows in the Bluebonnet Bar."

Tanner said, "You don't often find many to talk to in the Bluebonnet. It's the best saloon in Orejano, but the Apache crowd has sort of got folks scared of going there." He looked surprised.

Lena Lou asked curiously, "What were you talking about?"

"About a hawss," Caliper said noncommittally.

"What about a horse?" Tanner asked.

"There was an argument," Nogales said, "as to whether Hedge Furlow should ride a Circle-Slash pony — the one that brought him to town — or if he should use Trigger Ronson's hawss."

"Trigger Ronson?" Tanner frowned. "He and another feller have been hanging around Orejano a lot lately — feller named the Nevada Kid. I don't like their looks. But why should Furlow ride Ronson's bronc?"

"Straub Krouch didn't want him riding the Circle-Slash hawss," Caliper put in, eyes twinkling at the manner in which his listeners were being held in suspense.

"So Straub Krouch was in town, eh?" Tanner frowned. "I still don't see why Krouch shouldn't want Furlow to ride the Circle-Slash horse. Furlow works for the Circle-Slash."

"Not any more he doesn't," Nogales said.

"Is Furlow going away?" Tanner asked.

Caliper said, "He's gone — on Ronson's horse."

"But what's Ronson going to do?" Lena Lou asked.

"He's gone, too," Nogales grinned.

"Sounds like some sort of general exodus," Tanner said, puzzled.

"It was," from Caliper. "So Krouch rode back to the Circle-Slash, leading behind him Furlow's bronc and the horse of that other Circle-Slash hand, Cal Webster."

"Cal Webster left town, too?" Tanner frowned.

"He was going fast," Caliper chuckled, "the last reports we had."

"Sa-ay, what is this?" Tanner demanded. "Are you two ribbing us? You say Furlow's gone, Ronson's gone, Webster's leaving and — and — say, how about that other man, the Nevada Kid?"

"The Kid was one of the first to leave," Nogales said.

"Whose bronc did he leave on?" Tanner asked sarcastically. "You fellows are just full of information."

"The Kid didn't leave on a bronc," Caliper explained gravely. "He was pushed out of Orejano — on the fast, hot end of a lead slug."

"Oh-h," Tanner said, nodding, "I see. Those four fellows had a fight. I take it the slaughter was rather plentiful."

"Tell us about it," Lena Lou urged. "Did you see the fight?"

"Yeah, we saw it." Caliper nodded carelessly. "It was down at the Tip-Top Corral.

When it started Nogales was sitting on the top pole of the corral fence. You know how he is, always sitting around, waiting for something to happen. And then he got so excited he fell off into the corral, and his gun went off —"

"And just at that minute," Nogales cut in, "Caliper was coming in at the front end of the corral and, him being of an excitable nature, too, he reached for his gun —"

Tanner's coffee cup slammed suddenly against his saucer. "Jumpin' bull crickets!" he exclaimed. "*You boys* were in that fight!"

Caliper admitted modestly, "Yes, we played our small, insignificant part. Fate had decreed that Nogales and I —"

"— should lend" — Nogales took up the statement — "such aid as possible in extinguishing certain obnoxious forms of animal life at the time populating the Tip-Top Corral and —"

"Caliper! Nogales!" Lena Lou's knife and fork clattered against her plate. She said in some exasperation, "If you two boys aren't the darnedest! Here you've been in a fight and you come home and tell us you were listening to an argument about a horse. Of all things!"

Pablo and Tanner had also stopped eating. Pablo chuckled, "I'm theenk eet is a roundabout way of telling the tale — no?"

Tanner shook his head. "All right, you two,

you've had your joke. Now for heaven's sakes start at the beginning and tell us the story straight. Can't you see, it's like we're all sitting on cactus spines waiting for your yarn. Get talking, Nogales — Caliper — before I plumb explode from suppressed excitement."

So, eyes twinkling at first, Nogales and Caliper told the story, their voices becoming a trifle grave as they reached the end. When they had concluded there was a few moments' silence, then Tanner spoke:

"You've accomplished a good job, boys. It's my guess that both Ronson and the Nevada Kid were hired gunmen, killers, imported by Krouch."

"They'll never do any more killing," Caliper said soberly. "Last we heard, Webster was going fast. Hedge Furlow left town, of course. I don't reckon we'll ever hear of him again."

"Of course," Nogales added, "Krouch denied all knowledge of the affair. He came into the Bluebonnet afterward and pretended to be friendly. He bawled Furlow to a frazzle on the main street of Orejano. I think Furlow was about to tell, once or twice, what he knew about Krouch but was too afraid of Krouch's gun to speak out. Anyway, Krouch wouldn't even let him have the horse he'd been riding to leave town on. Furlow finally took Ronson's horse, and the last we saw of him he was fanning the dust out of Orejano."

Lena Lou shivered. "I don't like you boys risking your lives protecting my property," she said slowly.

"We weren't protecting your property," Nogales said. "Those four were spoiling for a fight, and we gave it to them."

Lena Lou shook her head. "I don't think it would have happened at all, if you hadn't been on my pay roll — if I can call it a pay roll when I don't pay anything." She smiled wistfully.

"Aw, forget it," Caliper said. "That's all in the day's work."

For an hour or so more they all sat and talked about the fight and of conditions on the range. Finally Tanner took up his sombrero and announced his intention of heading for his Maple-Leaf outfit. He said good night to Pablo and Lena Lou. Nogales and Caliper accompanied him down to the corral.

"This fight today," he said seriously, "doesn't mean the end of the trouble, boys. I figure this is only a starter. You've both got to keep your eyes peeled for danger. Krouch will be more dangerous than ever now. He won't be the sort to forget. You licked four of his men today and, besides, you broke Stan Cox's arms the other day. Krouch is about due, I figure, to try and even the score. He won't take defeat lightly."

"I don't care how he takes it," Nogales grinned, "just so long as he takes it."

"It's no laughing matter," Tanner replied. "I've tried to keep the Maple-Leaf clear of range battles, but from now on if you two need any help don't hesitate to let me know. The Maple-Leaf is at your service, and you can bank on every man on my pay roll."

"Thanks, Lee," Caliper said, "we may have to send up a yelp for help yet."

Nogales nodded. "Things are commencing to thicken up a bit. There's a break due some place."

Tanner said *"adios"* and climbed into his saddle, heading toward the trail that led to the Maple-Leaf. Nogales and Caliper walked slowly toward the bunkhouse. Nogales said, "There goes one white cowman."

Caliper nodded. "He sure is. I was half inclined to tell him about the ghost herd we saw the other night."

"Yeah, I thought of that too. I've been thinking things over, and, in case anything should happen to us, it would be best for him to know what we learned."

They entered the bunkhouse and lighted one of the oil lamps. Old Pablo put in an appearance a few minutes later. The three men talked for a time, then blew out the light, pulled off their boots and climbed into bed. In a short time all three were dozing; Pablo, in fact, was snoring loudly three minutes after his head touched his burlap pillow.

Some time before dawn Nogales awakened

Caliper. Caliper at once arose and dressed. The two moved quietly out of the bunkhouse so as not to awaken old Pablo. Down at the corral, where they were saddling up, Caliper said, "You're getting to be the dangedest hombre to pull a man out of bed in the middle of the night. What's up now?"

"I've been awake, on and off, all night," Nogales explained. "I've been thinking —"

"I knew something was wrong with you."

"Shut up if you want to hear what I'm going to tell you. It's this way, pard: we know we've got to expect trouble from Krouch. It can't be avoided. All right, why shouldn't we take the offensive before he gets started?"

"That's good strategy. He'll be sort of tipped back on his heels — mentally — after the way we cleaned his gun fighters yesterday. You figure to get to him while he's off balance."

"You get the idea. We'll have to work with Lee Tanner in this and with his men. I'd like to look over his crew. The best time to find the crew all together is while they're at breakfast, before they've saddled up and left for the day's work. And I figure it's time we told Lee what we learned about that ghost herd at Phantom Pass."

"In other words, we're making an early morning call on the Maple-Leaf outfit."

"You've hit it right on the nose. C'mon, hurry up with your saddle. You going to take all day?"

"It's not daylight yet." Caliper put one booted foot against his pony's ribs and pulled hard on the cinch. The pony grunted, and Caliper pulled another notch.

"Daylight's not far off."

The two cowboys climbed into saddles, walking their ponies until they were out of earshot of the Star-M; then touching spurs to their mounts' sides, they moved into a fast, ground-devouring lope across the range.

For some time they rode steadily in the direction of the Maple-Leaf. The stars paled from the sky, false dawn came and vanished. For a few moments the sky grew darker. Then a gray streak showed along the eastern horizon. The gray turned to red and then yellowish orange as the sun lifted above the hills, spreading its light across the surrounding country. Small birds commenced to move in the brush. Another day was born.

The morning breeze lifted across the range and whipped into the faces of the two riders. Caliper yelled once, across the intervening space between the loping horses, "Seems to take a long spell to reach the Maple-Leaf. Are you sure we're heading in the right direction, Nogales?"

Nogales nodded. "I don't figure we're much off the course. Follow me and you'll wear diamonds someday —"

"Or handcuffs," Caliper called back.

Before Nogales could find a fitting retort

there came to their ears the sound of a dishpan being vigorously beaten to accompany the long-drawn-out yell of a camp cook. "Grub pile, rannies! Come and get yore stuffin' before I throw it on the ground-d-d-d!"

The two cowboys spurred forward and topped a slight rise of ground. There, a short distance ahead and to the right, lay the buildings of Lee Tanner's Maple-Leaf outfit.

Nogales slowed pace just a moment to take in the neat, orderly array of buildings. He nodded with satisfaction then spurred forward. "C'mon, pard!" he yelled. "We're in time for breakfast, and I could eat anything that didn't bite me first. Let's go!"

And the two raced down the long slope, the sharp morning air lending a keen edge to their already healthy appetites.

14. An Attack Planned

Lee Tanner, on his way from his ranch house, spied Caliper and Nogales as they were on their way from the corral to the cookhouse. The Maple-Leaf boss hailed them, and they turned to wait for him to come up. They noticed Tanner wore a worried expression as he drew near, but he forced a welcoming smile.

"You're just in time for breakfast," he greeted. "You're out early this morning."

Nogales nodded. "We were just riding across the range, communin' with nature's birds and flowers, you might say, when Caliper heard your cook beating the pan. Well, food never did get past that cow-willie, so here we are."

"What's more, it's not going to," Caliper stated. "I always aim to eat regular when possible."

"And you don't often miss your aim," Nogales chuckled.

"All right, all right," Tanner smiled, "you've stalled me long enough. What really brings you out so early?"

"Oh, we were just taking the air for our health," Nogales grinned. "Caliper couldn't sleep so he woke me up and we went riding — like we did the other night when we went hunting ghosts — wait, Lee, you don't have to worry any. Everything was all right at the Star-M when we left. That's not what brought us out."

Tanner looked relieved then suddenly glanced sharply at the two. "Hunting ghosts? What do you mean? Here, sit down a minute." He drew the two down on a bench ranged along the outside wall of the cookhouse. Inside could be heard the clattering of dishes mingled with the voices of the Maple-Leaf crew. "What's all this about ghosts?" Tanner demanded. "And let's not have any of your ribbing for a spell. I never do know when to take you two seriously, though things have certainly moved since you hit this range."

"I meant what I said," Nogales replied, seating himself on the bench. "Somehow we couldn't take any stock in that ghost-herd yarn so we set out to investigate —"

"And, Mister Tanner," Caliper said, dropping down on the bench with his legs stretched out before him, "we sure hit the jack pot with our little investigation."

Tanner looked as though he were being made the butt of a joke. His next words sounded skeptical. "This is more of your ribbing, I suppose. Next thing I know you'll be telling me you saw — actually saw — that ghost herd."

170

"That's what I'm trying to tell you," Nogales said.

Tanner laughed scornfully. "Trying to kid me — you two?" he asked. "Let's forget it. There's food on the table inside," jerking his head toward the cookhouse. "I'll stand a little ribbing better after I get some chow under my belt. Come on and eat."

"No, wait a minute, Lee," Nogales said. His face was serious now. "This is a straight rope we're throwing. I'll convince you that we're speaking truth."

From that point on he took up the story of what he and Caliper had learned on their nocturnal visit to Phantom Pass a few nights previously. Tanner, at first skeptical, finally settled to listen in growing amazement.

". . . So you see," Nogales finally concluded, "it's a put-up job. Real ghosts don't run from a rifle shot. I figure it out — and Caliper agrees — that it's all a scheme to keep folks from snooping around the pass when there's stolen stock to be run across the border line. What's your slant in the matter?"

Tanner didn't say anything for a few minutes, then, "Well, you two have certainly called the turn. It looks like one slick scheme. But who's back of all this?"

"If your guess is the same as mine," Caliper said, "the coyote who's robbing this country blind of its stock and putting on that ghost parade is named Straub Krouch. Nogales and I have thought about the matter a heap. We can't think of anybody it might be but Straub Krouch."

"If it's not Krouch," Nogales asserted, "I'll eat my Stet hat!"

Tanner nodded. "I'd figure Krouch too." He frowned suddenly. "I wonder if they're planning to run any of my beeves across soon?"

"Have you lost some recent?" Caliper asked quickly.

Tanner nodded. "Yesterday — while I was visiting the Star-M instead of staying here and 'tending to business. I didn't learn about it until last night when I got home, after eating supper with you boys."

"How many did you lose?" Nogales asked. "Let's have the story."

Tanner explained: "I had a small bunch of thirty blooded cows I was keeping over near Tintos Creek. Kept 'em over there because I didn't want 'em mixing in with my crossbreeds in the main herd. Had one of my men, Bud Thompson, riding herd on 'em. Well, to cut a long story short, Bud doesn't know exactly what happened except suddenly he felt a terrific blow on the head. It knocked him cold. As he was losing consciousness he heard a gun report, and as near as he can figure it out he was shot at from a clump of brush some distance back of where he was sitting his saddle —"

"Didn't kill him, then?" Nogales looked relieved.

Tanner shook his head. "It was just luck he wasn't killed. The bullet just creased him a mite. I reckon he was left for dead. When Bud came to, his horse was still there, cropping grass, but there wasn't nary a head of stock left in sight. The rustlers had run the hoofs off'n 'em to get 'em out of the neighborhood, according to what Bud read of their sign after he regained consciousness. Bud was right groggy when he arrived home, so I don't know if he was able to do a good job reading the sign. I'd figured to go over there this morning myself."

"Might find something, but I doubt it," Nogales said. "Probably thought your cowpuncher was dead the minute he tipped out of his saddle. Being it happened in the daytime they wouldn't want to wait to investigate."

"No doubt that's how it was," Tanner agreed. "Bud came back here about supper time last night. The boys tell me he was right dizzy in the head. One of the other boys, not knowing where I was, went into Orejano looking for me, but of course I was at the Star-M. Anyway, Bud's feeling all right today, for which I'm thankful. Except for a scratch along one side of his head he's as right as ever. He wants to saddle up and go to work this morning, but I've insisted he take the day off to get over his headache."

"Good idea." Nogales nodded. "Working with a headache under a hot sun isn't always the best thing in the world for a man."

The flavor of food wafted through the open window of the cookhouse, and the rattle of dishes prompted Caliper's next remark. He said, grinning, "I've got a hunch we can talk as well with a knife and fork in our dewclaws as well as out here."

Tanner jumped to his feet. "Shucks! I plumb forgot about breakfast. Come on in and meet my outfit. They've heard about you and your fight with those four coyotes yesterday. Vinnie Dunlop — he's the boy who made the trip to Orejano, looking for me last night, after Bud Thompson was shot — Vinnie Dunlop brought back that news. The boys are feeling right friendly toward you already. It's time you said hello to 'em."

Tanner led the way into the cookhouse. Seated at a long table bearing platters of bacon, beans and potatoes, were five punchers, one of them with a bandaged head. At the kitchen door stood a grinning Chinese cook. The men glanced up as Tanner and the two cowboys entered.

"Gang," Tanner introduced, "these gentle lambs have arrived to wolf breakfast with us. Nogales Scott and Caliper Maxwell — shake hands with Bud Thompson — wearing that turban — Vinnie Dunlop, George Tilden,

Murray Cramm, Norman Perry — oh yes, and Ting Low, the best cook in this neck of the range, even if I do say it myself, as shouldn't, or he'll be asking for a raise. Ting Low, fetch some more dishes."

Nogales and Caliper shook hands all around. They liked the looks of the Maple-Leaf punchers. They looked capable, hard working, loyal to the core. The punchers eyed Caliper and Nogales with considerable admiration, prompted by the tales of their gun prowess. Ting Low scuffled out to return presently with more dishes and an extra coffee pot. Nogales and Caliper and Tanner found seats at the table. For several minutes nothing was heard except the rattle of crockery and tableware.

Finally the puncher named Murray Cramm could withhold his curiosity no longer; he wanted to ask questions about the fight with Trigger Ronson, the Nevada Kid and the other gunmen. That prompted questions from George Tilden and Norman Perry. The talk became general, and by the time breakfast was finished the Maple-Leaf punchers felt they'd known Caliper and Nogales for a long time. A strong friendship had already been established between the men.

Finally, breakfast was concluded and Ting Low commenced to pick up the dishes. Sacks of Durham appeared; cigarettes were rolled and lighted. Blue smoke drifted through the cookhouse and was wafted out the open doorway through which the morning sunshine streamed brilliantly.

Tanner opened the conversation, which had fallen off a trifle while the men were busying themselves with after-breakfast cigarettes. "Boys," Tanner stated soberly, "you all know I've been up against a tough proposition here. It wasn't helped yesterday when Bud was shot and those cows run off. Things have gradually been going from bad to worse — though I admit they've brightened a heap since Nogales and Caliper hit this part of the range. Some things have happened which I think will interest you. You've all heard of the ghost herd that —"

Considerable laughter broke out at the mention of the ghost herd. Norman Perry chuckled, "We've heard talk, but that talk's just to fool the Mexes hereabouts, I reckon. Naturally, nobody with the ability to figure things himself believes in that wild tale —"

"Why should anybody want to fool the Mexicans — or us, either, for that matter, Norm?" Tanner asked.

Norman Perry shrugged his lean shoulders. "You got me, Lee. I guess it's just an old superstition hereabouts that has hung on."

"Maybe you're wrong, Norman." Tanner smiled. "Boys, I'm going to ask Nogales and Caliper to tell you something they've discovered about that ghost herd — something that

I guarantee will make your eyes bug out with surprise. You want to listen close."

George Tilden exclaimed, "You're not aiming to make us believe there really is a ghost herd?"

"I didn't believe it myself at first," Tanner admitted ruefully. "Thought I was being kidded. But you can take Caliper's and Nogales' word for what happened." He turned to Caliper and Nogales, saying, "You can speak out. These boys are familiar with the rustling situation here, and I'll stake everything I own that every one of 'em is on the square. I brought 'em with me when I first came to the Maple-Leaf. I've known 'em for some years now so I know what I'm talking about. Since I've been acting in the capacity of both boss and foreman I've learned that they're more than just hired hands — they're pards who will back me — and you too — to the last ditch."

"That's quite a speech, Lee," Nogales smiled.

"It wasn't meant to be," Lee said soberly. "I just wanted you to know there isn't a hand here I wouldn't trust with my life."

"I'd already figured that much," Nogales said. "Well, cowpokes, here's the story. You may be inclined to laugh at first, but it's all straight goods — the real McCoy. . . . A coupla nights ago Caliper and I decided to go over and take a look at Phantom Pass and . . ."

Looks of astonishment formed on the faces of his listeners, as Nogales related his and Caliper's encounter with the Phantom Herd. When he had finished there was silence for several moments. Finally Bud Thompson, the cowboy with the bandaged head, broke the quiet.

"I never did take any stock in that ghost story, but it looks as though you two hombres have proved to our satisfaction that there's something to it after all. It looks to me as though you had the whole setup right well analyzed. There's only one thing left to do now — blast out this ghost herd gang, regardless whether it's Straub Krouch or somebody else is back of the gang. Me, I'm craving to get a whack at the snakes who creased my head yesterday. When do we start?"

Nogales looked from man to man and saw the same question forming on the lips of every puncher there. His heart leaped. He nodded with satisfaction. This was the sort of fighting, hard-riding crew he liked to have at his back — good fighters who could be trusted not to show the white feather no matter what the situation.

"Your words are plumb welcome, Bud," Nogales grinned. "I was hoping you boys would be craving a mite of action and ready to go on the prod after what I told you. If everybody's willing, we'll make a start tonight. Yesterday the Maple-Leaf lost thirty head of good stock. After the way Caliper threw lead at the ghosts I'm betting the rustler gang will be anxious to unload, as soon as possible, any stock it picks up. One thing is certain, I'm sure: the rustlers won't be happy until they can learn who fired that shot at their ghost parade."

"Have you anything planned now?" Lee Tanner asked.

"Nothing much," Nogales admitted, "but I'd like to go out to the hogback near Phantom Pass tonight. I've a hunch they might try to drive your animals through the pass into Mexico tonight. If they did, it would be a good thing to be on hand and put a stop to it. They might even have some other rustled cattle with 'em. If they do start driving stock through the pass, we could wait until they're well started and then drop down on 'em — plumb sudden. Take 'em by surprise."

"That sounds good to me." Tanner nodded enthusiastically. "We wouldn't have to leave here until near dark, then we could get to that hogback before the moon was up."

"That's a good idea. And we'll take plenty cartridges."

Tanner laughed shortly. "You don't have to tell my hands that."

They conversed a while longer, planning out details of the proposed attack on the rustling gang. Finally Nogales rose from the table.

Caliper looked surprised. "Where you going, pard?"

Nogales replied carelessly, "Oh, I thought I'd just ride into Orejano. I might even run across our good friend, Straub Krouch. Any friendly remarks I can pass on from you boys?"

A chorus of voices replied in a loud negative. Apparently Straub Krouch wasn't at all popular with the Maple-Leaf outfit.

Bud Thompson growled, "I never did have any use for Krouch, right from the first. We were all glad to know that you shot up his Apache Saloon that first day when you pulled Lee out of that tight he was in. None of us ever did trust Krouch or that dang Stan Cox that took his orders. You and Caliper had the whole Maple-Leaf's crew's thanks for that job well done. The Apache is just a dive for scum — nothing more. If there was any law and order in Orejano, the place would have been cleaned out long ago."

"By the way," Vinnie Dunlop broke in, "that's something I forgot to tell you before. We've been so occupied with Bud getting shot and the cows rustled that it slipped my mind. Orejano now has a deputy sheriff."

"That right?" Tanner asked. "I knew

there'd been some talk about having one here, but —"

"He arrived on the night stage when I was in town last evenin'." Vinnie nodded.

"What's his name?" one of the other punchers asked.

"Max Burgett got the job," Vinnie said.

"Him?" Tanner showed some surprise.

"You know him?" Nogales asked.

Tanner nodded. "Yeah, I know him," he said slowly. "He had the job of tax collector in this county. So the sheriff appointed Burgett, eh?" He laughed shortly.

Vinnie Dunlop said, "Burgett's reopened that old deputy office. I saw him messing around in there last night as I was leaving Orejano."

"What's the matter with this Burgett?" Nogales asked. "Is he crooked?"

Lee Tanner said slowly, "No, I don't figure Max Burgett as crooked. But he's kind of slow and easygoing. I don't see him as a peace officer. Still, you can't ever tell. He might pan out all right." He paused, snorting angrily, "That's the way politics run in this county. Dang those politicians at the county seat. The sheriff sits there in Arroyo Center on his fat rear end, knowing we should have an officer here. When it gets so he has to appoint one he gets a feller without any experience in that line a-tall. Those political hombres act as if they didn't give a dang for

181

their country. All they think about is keeping men of their own party in jobs. I know a dozen men would have made a better deputy sheriff than Max Burgett, but as luck would have it they belong to the other party. Hang politics, anyway!"

"Well," Nogales chuckled at Tanner's ill temper, "so long as you say Burgett isn't crooked maybe there's some hope for him. I reckon I might drop in and have a talk with him when I'm in town. Or I might run across Krouch. By accident Krouch might drop some mention of where he expects to be tonight."

"Why you so anxious to go to town, Nogales?" Caliper asked curiously. "And why you so interested in that new law officer?"

"Oh, nothing," Nogales replied lazily. "I was just wondering, that's all."

"I think you're a liar," Caliper said bluntly. "When you get that sleepy look in your eyes I can always tell you're cooking up something. Let me in on it."

The others looked curiously at the two. Nogales laughed and said, "T'tell the truth I had an idea in mind and —"

"Let me in on it," Caliper insisted.

Nogales shook his head. "I've got to play this hand alone, pard. You stay here and sun your worthless carcass against a wall. Catch up on your sleep; you'll be awake tonight, remember. Just wait for me until I get back.

Don't fret, you'll see plenty of action before this whole business is settled peaceful. I can't take you with me now because I'm headed on a mission that takes brains."

"There isn't any use of *you* going then," Caliper retorted indignantly. "I'm the proper man to go. . . ."

Meanwhile Lee Tanner was allotting to his men the various tasks of the day. He himself was going to ride with Vinnie Dunlop over toward the spot where the stolen cattle had been grazing. Bud Thompson, alone of the crew, remained at the ranch, much to his disgust. He insisted that he felt well enough to ride, but Tanner wouldn't hear of his working.

"You save yourself for tonight, cowboy," Tanner said. "There'll be plenty of work then for you to do — and most of it will be with gunpowder."

The punchers disappeared from the cook shanty and headed for the corral to saddle horses. Tanner was curious as to the reason for Nogales' trip to Orejano but he didn't ask any questions.

Finally only Bud Thompson, Ting Low — who was washing dishes by this time — Caliper and Nogales were left in the cookhouse.

"So you won't take me with you and you won't tell me why you're going, eh?" Caliper growled.

"Sorry, pard —" Nogales commenced.

"I got a good notion to go on my own hook," Caliper said defiantly.

"Go ahead," Nogales said. "Suckers always do."

Caliper frowned. "Suckers always do what?" he asked puzzled.

"Go on hooks — fishhooks," Nogales grinned.

Bud Thompson burst into laughter. Caliper's face grew red as he sought a devastating retort. But none would come. He could only stand and sputter.

"You sure bit on that one," Nogales laughed.

"Aw — aw — aw —" Caliper stammered.

But Nogales didn't hear that. He had already left the cookhouse and was on his way to the corral where he had left his horse. By this time the others had saddled up and were heading across the range in various directions. The sun was beating down, hot and brilliant, though a fresh breeze helped to hold down some of the heat.

Back in the cookhouse Bud Thompson asked, "What do you reckon Nogales aims to do in Orejano?"

Caliper shook his head, chuckling. "I haven't the least idea. But I can always tell when he's cooking up something. Lord knows what he's got in his head. I only asked to go with him just to devil him a mite. I knew he didn't want me. That settled that."

"But didn't you want to go?" Bud asked in amazement. Caliper shook his head again. "Nope, I've got a couple of ideas of my own. You're one of them."

"Me?" Bud's eyes opened wider beneath his head bandage.

"You. I don't hold with you doing any work today, like Lee said, but I don't reckon it will hurt if you and I take a little ride."

"I'm with you. Where we going?"

"I'll explain that later. Look around and find a Stet hat big enough to cover that bandage. A wound under a hot sun isn't so good to ride with sometimes, and if we're not lucky we might have to ride hard — and fast. And don't forget to carry a belt full of ca'tridges. We might need 'em!"

15. "Insist on Cash!"

Nogales was already on the road to Orejano about two miles from the Maple-Leaf when, struck by a sudden idea, he wheeled his pony from the trail and headed off across the range in the direction of the Star-M Ranch. He rode, deep in thought, sometimes frowning, at others, chuckling as a certain plan took form in his fertile brain.

"If it will only work," he muttered, "if it will only work. A lot will depend on . . ."

Then another phase of the plan struck him, and he broke into silent laughter. After a time the roofs of the Star-M buildings lifted into view.

Arriving at the ranch, Nogales dismounted from his pony and left its reins dangling on the earth. He saw Lena Lou just coming up from the barn with a supply of mesquite roots for the kitchen stove. She greeted him with a smile, looking above the armload of firewood.

"I figured as long as I was supposed to be working for you," he grinned, "I should show up here for a few minutes, anyway. Here, let me pack those roots for you."

The girl relinquished her load, and he took

it inside to the wood box then turned back and brought in several more loads. As he dumped the last load into the box, Lena Lou said, "Where's Caliper?"

"I left him at the Maple-Leaf. I'm heading for town in a few minutes. He pretended he wanted to go with me, but I could tell by the look in his eye that he had plans of his own." He gave the wood box a kick. "There, you've enough wood to cook a half-dozen chicken dinners like we had that first night."

Lena Lou smiled wistfully. "I don't reckon the old Star-M will be able to afford many more chicken dinners."

"Don't you be too sure of that now, girl," Nogales said quickly. "Don't count your chickens until they're snatched — clean out of reach. Where's Pablo?"

The girl gestured toward the east. "Over yonderly about a mile. He can see the house from there. He had a section of fence around a quicksand to mend. He said you had left the bunkhouse this morning before he was awake — just like you did a couple of mornings ago."

"We sloped over to see Lee Tanner this morning. I wanted to size up his crew. That was the best time to catch 'em all there — breakfast time."

"Is that where you were the other time?" Lena Lou asked.

"No ma'am, and you know that very well,"

Nogales laughed. "You're just fishing for information. As a matter of fact the other time we rode out looking for the ghost herd."

The girl thought he was kidding. "And of course," she said gravely, "you found it."

"Of course." He nodded. "Old Pablo isn't as superstitious as you figured him to be. He had a basis for what he said."

"Nogales! What are you talking about? I hope you're not trying to tell me you actually saw that ghost herd."

"Nothing else, lady."

The girl laughed. "Nogales! Can't you and Caliper ever be serious? You should know better than to think I'd believe that sort of tale. Now tell the truth, what did you come here for?"

"Can you ask?" Nogales said gallantly.

Lena Lou blushed. "Maybe we'd better keep on the subject of ghosts." She smiled.

"Maybe we'd better," Nogales gulped. There was something dazzling about Lena Lou's smile. "But what I told you about locating that herd is the truth."

"Now, Nogales — !"

He finally succeeded in convincing the girl and told her as briefly as possible what he and Caliper had discovered at Phantom Pass.

"Well, I never!" Lena Lou exclaimed. "Nogales, you've —"

Nogales cut in so as not to waste too much time over questions regarding the ghost herd, "Lena Lou, how much is the Star-M worth at present?"

The girl looked at him with wondering eyes. "Why, I just couldn't say offhand," she replied slowly. She pondered a minute or so. "Right now it isn't worth as much as it was before my father was killed — died. Repairs are badly needed, though you and Caliper have fixed a lot of things. But the best of the stock has been run off, and so — well, Straub Krouch offered me five thousand dollars for the place. Naturally that's downright robbery —"

"If Krouch offered you five thousand dollars," Nogales cut in quickly, "the Star-M is worth at least twenty thousand, just as it stands, for land and buildings. We can forget the stock for the present." He paused and considered a moment, then said, "Suppose I offered you thirty thousand dollars for the Star-M? Would you take it?"

The girl stared at him a moment. Then her eyes grew dreamy. "Thirty thousand dollars," she said slowly. "What I could do with thirty thousand dollars. . . ." Suddenly she exclaimed, "Man alive! Would I take thirty thousand dollars for the Star-M? Will a duck swim? Will a thirsty cow head for a water hole? Say, Nogales, if you offered that much money for my ranch, I'd take it so fast it would make your head swim."

"It wouldn't be the first time my head had

been in that condition," he grinned, "but not from the same cause."

The girl shook herself impatiently. "But you're just fooling. Where would you get thirty thousand dollars?"

"Oh, I might manage to scrape it up," Nogales said carelessly. "I could save here and do without things there, and so on — if I figured to raise the money. But it might not be necessary for *me* to raise the money. I was just trying to get a line on what you'd take."

The girl looked disappointed. "I thought you were just fooling. There I go — building air castles again."

"Don't be too sure," Nogales said. "If things will only work out, maybe we can put solid foundations under those air castles."

"No chance, cowboy," Lena Lou said hopelessly.

"Maybe I can't agree with you," Nogales said. "But now that we've got the price set at thirty thousand just remember that figure. Don't come down on it — not for anybody. And if anybody offers you that much, take it — but insist on cash!"

"Don't worry," she laughed. "I'd not only take it, I'd snatch it." She looked at him curiously. "What makes you think I might get an offer for the Star-M? What do you know that you haven't explained to me?"

"*Quién sabe?* Who knows?" he replied cryptically. "Maybe we can get Krouch to raise his offer."

Lena Lou's laugh held a trace of bitterness. "Not Straub Krouch, Nogales. You don't know that man like I do."

"Maybe not," he agreed. "But we'll see what we'll see. Meantime don't you forget that figure and what I told you — insist on cash!"

He picked up his sombrero and started to leave the kitchen. Lena Lou caught his arm, swung him around and studied his features.

"Nogales," she said earnestly, "wait! I don't understand. There's more to this than you've put into words. What idea are you working up now?"

Nogales looked into the girl's questioning eyes and found it difficult not to say more. He caught his breath a trifle, then answered, "I'm not ready to explain it all yet, Lena Lou. I haven't time to say more now. I've got to push on to Orejano. I'll see you later."

And with that he was gone and in the saddle, turning his pony out toward the trail before the girl could detain him any longer.

Lena Lou gazed after him for a long time until the cloud of dust raised by his pony's hoofs had disappeared from view.

"That man!" she said with some exasperation and then amended it to, "Those men! A body never can figure what they're working out!"

16. Nogales Mixes with the Deputy

Nogales took it easy on the trip into Orejano. It seemed ever since he had hit this country he'd been working his pony hard in one direction or another. He'd lost a bit of sleep himself, come to think of it; too many sleeping hours had been filled with thinking, when he should have been resting. Most of the trip into town Nogales dozed in the saddle.

At that, it was well before noon when he rode into Orejano. He stopped first at the Bluebonnet Bar. Johnnie Armstrong stood behind his bar. There weren't any customers there at present.

"Bottle of beer, Johnnie," Nogales greeted, striding into the barroom. "What's the matter, trade fallen off a mite?"

Johnnie set out a bottle and glass. He said, frowning, "Straub Krouch came into Orejano this morning. He's spread it all over town that anybody who fails to patronize his Apache Saloon won't stand very high with him. Well, Krouch swings just enough influence to affect my trade. But I'll still get the better class of people. It's a mite early for them to drink yet."

"I was wondering if Krouch would be in town this morning," Nogales said meditatively, pouring his beer and watching the creamy suds rise above the amber liquid in the glass.

"Yeah, he's in town," Johnnie grunted. "Somebody mentioned a spell back that he's making an inventory at the Apache, trying to figure out just what he'll have to buy new to replace the stuff you boys smashed the other day when you cleaned out that joint."

"I feel awfully sorry about that," Nogales chuckled.

"Yes, you do — in a pig's eye."

"How's the new deputy working out, Johnnie?"

"Max Burgett? He'll be all right, I reckon, if he can ever learn to stir his stumps. He's a bit heavy in the wrong places — some people might call it lazy. At the same time I figure him honest and anxious to make a good showing, if he had a chance. But the whole county figures that Straub Krouch is running Orejano, and there isn't much can be done."

"Maybe that can be changed, too," Nogales said grimily.

He finished his beer and started out.

"Leaving so soon?" Johnnie Armstrong asked.

Nogales nodded. "You'll be hearing of me soon again, I hope. S'long, see you later, Johnnie."

Johnnie said, "S'long," and Nogales left the Bluebonnet and again climbed into his saddle. Down the street, the distance of a city block to the east, beyond the Tip-Top Corral a few doors, Nogales saw above a squat, adobe structure a sign bearing the words: *Deputy Sheriff — Orejano County.* The sign had been there a long time from all appearances. One glance at the windows of the building showed Nogales that the office wasn't often occupied. One window was cracked; the others dirty and grimed.

Nogales dismounted at the ancient, much gnawed hitch rail before the deputy sheriff's office and headed toward the open door of the building. Suddenly he halted. From within the office came a sound that greatly resembled that made by a boiler letting off steam. In short, someone was sleeping rather noisily.

Nogales peered around the corner of the doorway. There sat Deputy Sheriff Max Burgett, sprawled back in his desk chair, spurred boots propped on the desk before him. He was a bulkily built man with thinning hair. His mouth was wide open, his eyes closed, his head tilted to one side against the high back of the chair. Buzzing flies played hide-and-seek in his open mouth, seemingly undisturbed by the deep-throated snores which at regular intervals filled the air.

Nogales, standing in the open doorway,

194

laughed noiselessly. He glanced along the front wall of the building where two Mexicans slouched in the dust, their backs resting against the adobe office. Both were occupied with a pair of dice, engrossed in a game in which no stakes were visible. They had paid no attention to Nogales when he stepped to the doorway of the office. Their heads didn't raise now.

"Probably just throwing those galloping dominoes for the fun of it," Nogales mused. "At any rate I don't figure they're going to be interested in what goes on in here — not right away, at least."

He tiptoed into the office, moving cautiously so as not to arouse the sleeping deputy sheriff. The interior of the office was small, with a door, at present closed, leading into a larger room at the rear. This larger room was partitioned off into jail cells, now empty of occupants.

"I could have guessed it would be empty," Nogales chuckled noiselessly. "This snoring deputy advertises that fact."

The office was extremely dirty. Dust was everywhere. A worn saddle lay in one corner near a weathered valise. A rifle rested on wooden pegs on one wall. Several fly-specked maps and reward dodgers, faded yellow, were stuck at random about the cracked plaster walls. Each of the reward dodgers, or "Wanted Bills," as they were often known, furnished a description of some culprit whose apprehension was desired by the law, and at the bottom, in bold black type, was the amount offered for capture. Some carried photographic reproductions of much wanted law breakers.

Nogales moved softly about the room, studying the reward dodgers. At last he found what he'd been looking for, a bill unillustrated and carrying a description much akin to his own. Here the sum of $1500 was offered for the body, "dead or alive," of one Jack Anderson, "better known as Red Anderson, alias Andy Redmond, alias The Sundown Slasher."

Nogales' gaze swiftly perused the printed words, *Wanted for various crimes, the latest being the murder of Sheriff Carstairs, Otera County, and the robbery of the Otera City Savings Bank* . . . Then followed the description: . . . *six feet tall, weight about 175* . . . *red hair* . . . *gray eyes* . . . Nogales whistled softly and broke off a moment, musing, "They sure come close with that description."

He read on, *Beware of Anderson* . . . *fast as lightning with his gun* . . . *a born killer* . . . *peace officers are warned not to take chances* . . . *shoot to kill, on sight* . . . Nogales gulped a trifle as he came to the end of the bill. "There's a heap of folks I wouldn't want to read this and then look at me. I'd be plumb li'ble to be taking a harp lesson from ol'

Saint Peter before I'd even learned all the hymns here on earth."

He hesitated just a moment, however, then reached up and jerked the reward bill loose from the wall. Turning, he strode across the room and waved the bill in the face of the sleeping deputy sheriff.

For a moment Deputy Max Burgett didn't stir, then, as Nogales drew the paper lightly across the sleeping man's face, he opened his eyes, stared bewilderedly about, yawned, then suddenly straightened up in his chair. As his gaze fell on the grinning Nogales, the booted feet jerked off the desk and landed with a thud on the floor.

"Huh-huh! What is it?" Burgett rubbed his eyes and looked a trifle sheepish. "Didn't expect to fall asleep. I was up most of the night, trying to get things in order around here, but the job seems endless. What's on your mind? What can I do for you, mister? Are you sure it's me you want to see? I'm the new deputy sheriff here. Name's Burgett — Max Burgett. Appointed by the sheriff —"

Nogales broke in, looking down at the deputy and chuckling, "Yeah, it's you I'm looking for. I'd like to talk to you a minute, if you'll come awake."

Burgett smiled guiltily. "I must confess I was asleep on the job —"

"Is that so?" Nogales said politely. "I'd never guessed it. But then, we all have our weaknesses. Maybe yours is lots of sleep."

"This climate is enough to make anybody sleepy. Over to Arroyo City, where I've been living, it's a mite cooler, and — well, you're not interested in that. What can I do for you?"

"Look this over." Nogales tossed the reward bill on the desk in front of Burgett.

Burgett glanced sharply at the bill then back to Nogales. "You know where this man can be found?" he asked quickly.

"I didn't say that. Read the description and then tell me if it fits anybody you've seen in your long and varied career as a peace officer."

"You've got me wrong there, mister. I'm new at this business. First time I've ever had a badge." Burgett smiled. "Just between you and me I don't know a great deal about it, how to go at things and so on. Of course I want to do my duty and enforce the law, so if you know where this man can be found —"

"Hadn't you better read this description first? The feller might be a heap nearer than you figure on."

Burgett looked at Nogales, frowned and then gazed at the paper before him, following the lines of small print with a stubby forefinger as he commenced to read slowly. Nogales stood above him, a sardonic smile on his features, watching Burgett closely.

Suddenly Burgett looked up, his eyes shifting to Nogales' head. "You've got reddish sort of hair," he said abruptly.

Nogales nodded. "Yeah, I have," he drawled. "It was a birthday present from my parents. I've had it ever since."

"We-ell," Burgett said uncertainly, his eyes shifting to various parts of Nogales' anatomy. There was a growing agitation in his manner. He started to speak, his eyes widening, his mouth closed again. Then, to throw Nogales off guard, he once more dropped his gaze to the printed page.

Almost at the same instant his eyes flashed up again, his six-shooter was jerked out of holster.

The move came too late. Nogales had out-guessed him, bringing his own weapon to bear on the deputy's form a split second before Burgett's six-shooter left its holster.

"Steady, Burgett, steady," Nogales warned. "I've got the drop on you. Don't try anything foolish." At the same time the ominous click of Nogales' gun hammer lent emphasis to the words.

The deputy sheriff stared into the muzzle of Nogales' .45, swore suddenly with irritation, then reluctantly shoved his own gun back into holster.

"You got me licked," he growled. "Why do you come here and give yourself up this way and then throw down on me? What's your game, Anderson?"

"I want to make *habla* with you a few minutes," Nogales said cheerfully.

"Well, go ahead, start your talk then," Burgett said angrily. "But, s'help me, the first chance I get —"

"Take it easy, like I advised you. I can't talk comfortable while you insist on keeping your fist wrapped on that six-shooter butt."

"That's exactly where my fist stays," Burgett snapped. "You can blast me or not, as you see fit. I'm warning you I'll do the same if I get a chance. I'm not letting go my holt on this gun and I'm using it first chance —"

"All right, all right," Nogales cut in regretfully, "if you see it that way, you see it that way. I was hoping we could have our talk comfortable, but if you insist on taking that attitude, there's nothing for me to do but keep you covered while I make my spiel. You see, I've got business in this neck of the range for a while, and I didn't want you to read that reward bill and then see me on the street before we'd come to some sort of agreement —"

"Red Anderson," Burgett declared angrily, "I'm not open to any bribes, so if you're figuring to buy me off while you're operating in this district you're just wasting your time. If possible I'll collect that reward offered for your capture. Don't make any mistake about that. I may not know much about this business, but I do know that law and order is needed bad in Orejano and I aim to do my best to enforce it."

"That's just lovely." Nogales smiled thinly. "I always like to meet an honest peace officer. Then we both know just where we stand —"

"Cut the talk," Burgett growled, "and get on with the business that brought you here."

Nogales nodded. "We're both clear on that point then. You're going to try and collect the fifteen hundred reward offered for the body of Red Anderson. At the same time I'm going to do my best to prevent you from shooting me. Just to make sure you don't try anything reckless, I'm going to keep you covered until I can persuade you" — the words came softly now — "to do me a little favor. In return I'm aiming to do you a favor. . . ."

The two Mexicans playing with the dice against the wall of the deputy's office had paid no attention to Nogales when he entered the doorway, though one of them had recognized the fighting *gringo* who had taken a part in the Tip-Top Corral battle the previous day. They could hear voices inside but couldn't distinguish what was being said even if they had been interested.

Eventually, they tired of the dice and settled their backs against the wall to accomplish a little peaceful dozing in the shade. Their eyes grew heavy and finally closed.

201

One of them even started a long-drawn snore when the interruption came.

Inside the deputy sheriff's office there came the loud, crashing explosion of a .45 gun. Two more shots thundered out in swift succession. From within the office came the voices of cursing men — scuffling feet — the sounds of a struggle. A heavy thud, as of a body striking the floor, followed another roaring exchange of shots!

In considerable trepidation the two Mexicans rose from their resting place and scurried for shelter. No telling when a stray bullet might fly through a window or penetrate a wall.

There was a loud yell, and Nogales emerged from the deputy's doorway with the speed of a cannon ball shot from a cannon. Without pausing in his stride, his long legs cleared the tie rail where he had left his horse, then he whirled and, without touching stirrup, vaulted into the saddle.

The pony's head came up with a jerk as it pivoted on hind legs. Half turning, even as the horse moved away from the tie rail, Nogales sent another shot crashing into the office doorjamb as he threw spurs to his pony's sides. In one jump the wiry cow pony was under way, flashing down the street in a swiftly moving cloud of dust.

Nogales had almost reached the eastern limits of Orejano when Deputy Sheriff Max

Burgett, covered with dust and disheveled as to clothing, came plunging out of his office, carrying his Winchester. Snapping the rifle to shoulder, he sent shot after shot winging in pursuit of the fleeing rider. None of the shots found their mark, apparently, as Nogales kept going without a pause. The next instant he had disappeared around a bend in the roadway, where it widened and spread out across the surrounding rugged country.

At the noise of the shooting people commenced to pour from doorways. In no time at all a goodly sized crowd had gathered about the office of the deputy sheriff. Straub Krouch had appeared at the door of the Apache at the first sound of gunfire and had seen Nogales come dashing from the deputy's office and flee down the street. His mouth fell open as he watched Nogales disappear from view with Burgett's rifle bullets speeding the retreat.

Now Krouch came running down the street to join the group gathered before Burgett's office. The men there were all talking at once in excited voices and with much waving of hands.

"What's wrong, Burgett?" Krouch demanded. "You have some trouble with that cowpuncher?"

"Cowpuncher, hell!" Burgett panted, red faced. "That's Red Anderson, bandit, murderer and —"

"Red Anderson?" Krouch exclaimed blankly. "I understood his name was Nogales Scott."

"Nogales Scott!" Burgett said scornfully. "I suppose that's what he told you. That's just another alias, probably. But he's Red Anderson, all right, alias Andy Redmond, alias The Sundown Slasher — and Gawd knows how many other fake names he's been traveling under. Right now he's wanted in Otera County for bank robbery and murder. And there was other crimes before that. Anderson's bad. Regular killer. Has a reputation for fooling folks into thinking he's just a lazy cowpuncher but he's a bad customer to monkey with —"

"How come he was in your office?" Krouch asked.

"There's reward bills out on him," Burgett explained. "I was warned against Anderson before I came to Orejano. There were rumors he was in this section of the country. He don't like those reward bills nohow and he's been going around destroying them whenever possible. I was asleep — that is, I was out back in my jail and when I came into the office he was just tearing a reward bill off my wall. The minute he saw me he was sure surprised and started shooting. I guess he'd figured I wasn't around. I was as surprised as he was, and we were shooting together. It's just luck I was able to get behind my desk so

I wa'n't hit. I closed with him, and that prevented him getting a good shot at me. Somehow I got knocked down and he got away. I reckon my bullets missed him complete, like his did me. I figure I'm lucky."

"How much reward is offered for his capture?" Krouch asked.

"Fifteen hundred dollars, dead or alive," Burgett replied promptly.

Krouch looked surprised and whistled softly. "That hombre sure must be bad. What you going to do about him?"

"We-ell" — Burgett looked a trifle reluctant — "I suppose my duty calls me to get on his trail. I'd sort of like to form a posse to go with me, but I'm warning everybody here that Red Anderson will never be taken alive without rubbing out two or three hombres to take with him. So you fellows that volunteer to go with me had better remember that."

He waited a moment. Nobody volunteered to join the posse. Instead, the crowd commenced to break up and go about its business. Only a half-dozen men remained now.

Burgett said contemptuously, "Guts seem to be at a premium in this town. Ain't there nobody got the nerve to help me with a posse?" Nobody answered. "I suppose some of you fellows figure you'll see him again, some place, and plug him in the back for the reward. Well, forget it. They say Red Anderson has eyes in the back of his head. That shooting from behind has been tried before, but, somehow, Anderson always seems to shoot first and leave a corpse behind him when he rides off. The man's dangerous!"

The rest of the crowd had disappeared by this time. Left now was only Krouch to talk to the deputy. Burgett said, "Well, I'm glad to see everybody in this town hasn't lost his nerve. You'll go with me, eh, Krouch?"

"Me?" Krouch looked startled. Then he shook his head. "Not me. It's not a matter of nerve. I'm just too busy. I've got business to straighten out at the Apache. On top of that I've got my Circle-Slash to operate. I haven't any time to be gallivanting around the country trying to capture Red Anderson. I tell you, Burgett" — and Krouch smiled nastily — "you capture Anderson singlehanded, then you'll have the whole reward to yourself."

"It looks as if that's what I'll have to do," Burgett said reluctantly.

Nearly twenty minutes had elapsed since Nogales had ridden out of Orejano. Burgett didn't appear very eager to get on the trail. Finally, muttering something about getting started, he heaved a long sigh and started reluctantly back into his office. Krouch looked after him a minute, then returned to the Apache, where a crowd had gathered to talk about the notorious Red Anderson.

A little later Max Burgett emerged from his

office, fully armed with two six-shooters and his Winchester. Carrying a canteen and saddles he headed toward the livery stable to get his horse. Arriving at the livery stable, more time was lost while he repeated the story of his encounter with Red Anderson to the livery man.

Altogether it was a full hour after the fight in his office, before Deputy Sheriff Max Burgett mounted his pony and rode out of town on Nogales' trail.

17. "I've Got You Covered!"

As Deputy Sheriff Max Burgett left the eastern limits of Orejano, Nogales came loping in at the western end of town. There were only a few people abroad by this time, and, while the report quickly ran through the town that Red Anderson had returned to Orejano, such was the impression gained through Burgett's warning against Anderson's gun prowess that no one cared to try to collect that fifteen-hundred-dollars' reward.

Straight down the center of the street Nogales rode, his eyes alert for the first hostile sign on either side. He noticed now that such men as he passed avoided his gaze. One or two may have been tempted to throw lead at that defenseless back, but memory of Nogales' set, determined face quickly thrust the idea from their minds. Somehow Nogales seemed able to see in every direction at once, and no one, apparently, cared to face his unerring aim.

Straight to the Apache Saloon Nogales rode. Here he dismounted and tossed a silver dollar to a Mex boy standing near. "Hold this *caballo* ready for a few minutes, *amigo*," he snapped tersely. "I may have to leave in a hurry."

The Mexican boy, round eyed, gulped and nodded and seized the reins of the pony.

A few moments later Straub Krouch received one of the great shocks of his life when Nogales came sauntering into the Apache Saloon, his spurs clanking musically on the bare flooring. The place was filled with customers at the moment, all talking at once. Someone caught sight of Nogales, said something in an undertone. The word spread from lip to lip. Gradually a silence fell over the Apache.

Nogales stopped a few yards just inside the entrance. One hand rested lightly on gun butt as he gazed at the men facing him from the bar. A thin smile crossed Nogales' face; a smile that held considerable contempt. He drawled softly, "Anybody here got ideas about collecting a reward?"

No one replied. No one made even the slightest motion toward his gun. Finally the men at the bar, with one accord, turned back to their drinks and commenced talking of subjects that bore no relation whatever to bandits.

Straub Krouch alone had moved to the center of the room and stood eyeing Nogales a bit defiantly.

"Well?" Nogales said.

Krouch asked sarcastically, "Didn't I see

you burning the wind out of Orejano a spell back?"

"You might have," Nogales grinned, "if you were looking my way at the time. I wasn't taking time to pick any flowers along the road as I passed, either."

"I noticed that," Krouch replied. He hesitated. "What say you and me have a drink?"

"I could do with a drink."

Krouch spoke to Mike Artora, presiding behind the bar. Artora pulled a cork from a bottle and placed it, with two glasses, on a tray which he handed to Krouch. Krouch took the tray and led the way to a table in one corner. Here the two men seated themselves, Nogales taking the seat with the back to the corner wall to Krouch's disappointment.

Krouch said, "You needn't be leery of getting shot in the back. While you're drinking with me you're under my protection. Nobody won't try anything."

"I'd just as soon not risk anything," Nogales said cheerfully. "From this seat I can watch the whole room, and nobody can get behind me. I figure it's safer that way."

Krouch shrugged his shoulders and poured two drinks from the bottle. "Regards," Krouch said, lifting his glass.

"*Salud!*" from Nogales. They drank. "That Old Crow is right smooth bourbon, Krouch," Nogales said, as he set his glass back on the table.

"It ought to be." Krouch nodded. "I pay enough for it. But then I always figure the best is none too good for a white man. None of this *mescal* for me. I'll leave that to the greasers."

"Meaning," Nogales said softly, "that you'll have greasers working for you but won't mix with 'em otherwise?"

"Just what are you hinting at?" Krouch asked sharply.

Nogales shrugged; his face was bland. "I'm not hinting at anything in particular. Your bartender is what I'd call a greaser. . . . But what's on your mind?"

Krouch looked narrowly at Nogales for a moment, then decided the words carried no hidden meaning. "I was mistaken," he said a bit nervously. "I thought you meant I had greasers handling cows for me — er — breeds — that is — hell! Let's forget it."

"There's no reason for me to remember it." Nogales smiled.

Krouch still looked a trifle uneasy. He changed the subject suddenly. "What was the trouble you was having with Max Burgett?"

Nogales grinned. "Didn't that deputy sheriff tell you?"

"Not a thing," Krouch lied. "He fiddled around some and tried to raise a posse to go on your trail with him but no luck. You can thank me for that. I sort of persuaded the boys from going. You know, I always liked you —"

"Thanks," Nogales cut in dryly. "Let's not open any Mutual Admiration Society until we determine we can do each other some good."

Krouch's face reddened. "Anyway," he growled, "Deputy Burgett rode out alone on your trail just a short time before you came in here. But what was the trouble between you two?"

"You're not curious, are you?" Nogales laughed shortly. "Well, to tell the truth Burgett had me confused with some other hombre with a price on his head. I just happened to be going past his office this morning and, seeing his door open, I wandered in to look over his reward bills. I like to collect unusual bills. It's sort of a hobby of mine —"

"A hobby that pays profits?" Krouch said meaningly.

Nogales shrugged. "I'm just interested in that sort of literature. Burgett woke up while I was there and mistook me for somebody else. He was asleep in his chair when I went in, and I reckon the sudden awakening sort of confused his mind. Anyway, he went for his gun and I went for mine. I didn't try to hit him — just wanted to scare him off. We had a bit of a tussle, so I figured I'd better fan the wind before somebody got hurt. That's all there was to it. I reckon he isn't awake yet 'cause I waited outside of town until I see him take up my trail, then I circled around and came in at the other end of Orejano."

"What sort of reward bill was it you were looking at when Burgett caught you?" Krouch asked, watching Nogales narrowly. "Whose name was on it?"

"I disremember," Nogales said promptly.

Krouch smiled scornfully. "Sometimes it pays to have a bad memory."

"Yeah, it does," Nogales drawled.

"If you ain't the damnedest fool!" Krouch swore softly and yet with a certain admiration in his tones. "To be looking in a deputy sheriff's office for reward bills — of all places. I've got a hunch that Burgett hasn't much ambition, but he's likely to jump into action plumb fast if he sees a chance to collect a reward right under his nose. You should have realized that."

"Haven't I told you," Nogales growled impatiently, "that Burgett was mistaken? He thought I was somebody else."

Krouch dropped one eyelid in a sly wink. "Sure, sure, Mister *Nogales Scott,* I believe you. Let's say no more about it."

"That suits me," Nogales said shortly. He changed to a fresh topic of conversation. "That first day I met you you mentioned something about giving me a job on your Circle-Slash outfit. Me, I'm sort of shy of cash at present, and as there isn't any savings bank in Orejano I'll have to —" he paused suddenly and bit his lip.

Krouch smiled nastily. "Now what would you want a savings bank in a town this size for?"

"Never mind that," Nogales said testily. "I'm just hankering to go to work for a spell. You may not believe it, but I've always drawn top hand's pay. I've even got letters of recommendation from men I've worked for in the past to prove it — wait, I'll show 'em to you." He broke off and commenced to fumble in an inner pocket of his vest.

"Where's that pardner of yours?" Krouch asked.

"Who, Caliper?" Nogales swore suddenly and ceased looking for his letters. "That mealymouthed saint is no pardner of mine. He's so good butter won't melt in his mouth. He was even wondering if there was a church he could go to in Orejano," Nogales said disgustedly. "We split up. Everything is sweet light and charity with that hombre. That's what we had the fight about — him and his charitable ideas. He's staying on at the Star-M s'far as I know — working without pay. When I left he even offered to shake hands and say he'd forgive me for my hard words. Phaugh!" Nogales spat angrily on the floor.

"You did right to split up, I reckon," Krouch said, "if Maxwell is that sort of hombre. You'd been pardners for a long time, though, hadn't you?"

Nogales shook his head and resumed his search for the letters of recommendation. "No, I just picked him up in Wyoming about a year ago. I had hopes for him at first, but, would you believe it? — the dang fool is willing to *work* for wages. I tell him he'll never get rich that way."

"He sure won't," Krouch agreed.

Nogales finally produced a handful of letters and miscellaneous papers, all jumbled together. "Now let's see, where's those letters," he muttered, thumbing over the pile.

As he searched through the papers for the letters of recommendation, one paper became detached from the group, slipped from his hand and sideslipped through the air to fall on the floor near Krouch's right foot. It happened to be a reward notice offering fifteen hundred dollars for the capture of one Red Anderson.

For a moment Nogales didn't notice the paper as it fluttered to the floor, then with undue haste he stooped to retrieve it. But Krouch had moved swiftly to get it first and straightened back in his chair, the paper in hand.

"Here, give me that," Nogales snapped. "That's something personal."

"Just a minute, feller," Krouch put him off, spreading the bill on the table before him and reading swiftly. "*Hmmm!* Reward dodger, eh? . . . Red Anderson . . . wanted for murder and bank robbery . . ."

Before Krouch had time to read further Nogales' gun was out. "Krouch," he said tensely, "I've got you covered under the table right now. Give me that paper — or else!"

Krouch hesitated, looked into Nogales' blazing eyes and decided to obey orders. Reluctantly, he folded the paper and shoved it across the table but he had already read enough to convince him that Nogales was one bad *hombre*. Nogales stretched one hand across the table, seized the bill and jammed it into his holster. Then he put his gun away. "Next time that bill comes out, Krouch," he said coldly, "my six-shooter comes out first. Remember that!" He leaned back in his chair, hand still gripping gun butt.

Krouch laughed a bit nervously and said, "Relax, *hombre*, relax. I'm not looking for trouble with *you*."

Nogales nodded shortly. "You're wise," he sneered. He shoved a couple of dog-eared letters across the table. "Here's those recommendations I spoke of."

Krouch guffawed, suddenly scornful. "Huh, feller, I don't want to waste time looking at those. I've already seen your recommendation. That's enough for me."

"Well, what you aiming to do about it?" Nogales said, somewhat sulkily.

Krouch's lips spread in a hateful grin. "Well, Mister *Red Anderson*," he replied, "I'm aiming to give you a job, like I said I would.

I'm not the type that holds a man's past life against him and turns him over to the law — not so long as he and I get along comfortable without any disagreements —"

"Forget that Red Anderson name." Nogales' eyes had narrowed to thin slits, and the words came sullenly. "My name's Nogales Scott — and don't you forget it."

"All right, Nogales," Krouch laughed good-naturedly. "I'll put you on my pay roll and pay you good wages. There'll be a bonus above wages if you can obey strict orders —" He broke off suddenly, struck by a new thought. "Say — what was that talk that day I met you about Lena Lou Morley getting a legacy or coming into some money or something?"

Nogales shook his head, frowning. "I'm not just sure what that was all about. She's flat broke now, but I've got a hunch there's something in the wind —"

"What is it?" Krouch was suddenly suspicious.

"I don't know. I must have been mistaken."

"You've changed your tune too suddenly, Nogales. You know something. You're holding out on me."

"I tell you I'm not."

Krouch spoke harshly, "All right, have it your way. If you won't talk, maybe I can't make you but I can try damned hard. Nogales, I've got *you* covered under the table *now!* Will you talk, or have I got to pull trigger?"

18. Krouch Plans a Double Cross

Nogales gazed across the table into the angry, bloodshot eyes boring into his own. "You're jumping to conclusions too fast, Krouch," he said steadily. "This is something we've got to talk over."

"You'll talk, all right," Krouch rasped. "Either that, or I'm pulling trigger."

"You'd commit murder — in here?" Nogales said.

Krouch's yellow teeth were bared in a snarl. "Why not in here?" he demanded harshly. "Deputy Burgett is out of town. Even if he wasn't, who cares about the life of Red Anderson, already with a price on his life? You can't figure on any of those hombres at the bar cutting in. There isn't a man among 'em who won't do as I say. So it's up to you, cow hand. Either you talk, or —"

"I tell you," Nogales commenced reluctantly, "that I —"

"Don't lie to me. I remember that day I met you Tanner acted awfully funny, trying to cover up something. What's he got under his bonnet?"

"His hair."

"Don't try to get funny," Krouch snarled

impatiently. "Don't forget I've got you covered under the table. Can you think of any good reason why I shouldn't shoot you?"

"Just one," Nogales said promptly.

"Meaning you'll talk?" Krouch said eagerly.

Nogales shook his head. "You'd get shot, too," he explained.

"I'd get shot!" Krouch's eyes opened wider.

"Uh-huh." Nogales nodded. "The force of your bullet might shock my trigger finger into action — and at present my trigger finger is pressing easy around the trigger of my six-shooter —"

"Wha— wha— wha—" Krouch stammered, going white. "Did — did — you —"

"I was a jump ahead of you, Krouch," Nogales grinned. "I saw you were working up to something so I just slipped my gun out a trifle before you did. So we're both covered. Now what you aiming to do?"

A sickly grin crossed Krouch's face. "It looks like a deadlock, doesn't it?" he quavered.

"Not as far as I'm concerned," Nogales replied carelessly. "I'm comfortable."

"Now look here, Nogales, we've got to talk this over —" Krouch commenced.

"I suggested that same thing a few minutes ago, if you'll remember."

"We-ell, you put your gun away and I'll do the same."

"I don't trust you yet, Krouch. You put

219

both your hands on the table first." Krouch hesitated. Nogales said sharply, "Go on, get those dewclaws in full view."

Krouch put his gun away and then placed both hands on the table. Nogales followed suit. Nogales said, laughing, "Now we're both back where we started."

"Except," Krouch said angrily, "that I don't reckon I'll give you a job now."

"Maybe not," Nogales said, "but you'll listen to me *habla* a mite, anyway. I've offered to talk this thing over with you. Just because I didn't tell you right off all I knew, you jumped to conclusions I was holding out on you. Under the circumstances, with so many people in here, you can't expect me to spill what I know. Nobody's paid any attention to us yet, but some fellers have mighty long ears —"

"Lena Lou has got some money coming then?" Krouch said eagerly.

"I'm still not talking," Nogales said bluntly. "Not in front of a barroom full of men."

Krouch jerked impatiently around in his chair and faced the bar. "You hombres clear out of here for a spell," he ordered loudly. "Me and Nogales Scott has business to talk over."

The men at the bar glanced around, then turned back and gulped their drinks. Within two minutes the place was empty of customers. Only Mike Artora remained behind the bar.

"You, Mike," Krouch ordered, "you get outside. Tell anybody that starts in for a drink that we're closed for a spell and don't let 'em through the doorway. D'ye hear me?"

"I'm hear you, Señor Krouch." The half-breed nodded respectfully and left the bar-room to take up a position just beyond the swinging doors.

Krouch swung back to Nogales. "That satisfy you?"

Nogales nodded. "The air's sweeter, anyway."

"Let's hear you talk now."

Nogales hesitated — just long enough to make his words carry the proper amount of weight. "Krouch," he said seriously at last, "for the present let's forget anything that may have been said by Tanner or anybody else that day I met you. I've got my faults but I never yet broke my word to anybody. That's why I don't want to talk about that day —"

"I get you, I get you," Krouch said impatiently. "What are you going to tell me? Never mind what you promised Tanner you wouldn't tell —"

"I didn't say I'd promised Tanner anything. I merely started to tell you I'd never broke my word to anybody that was square with me —"

"All right, all right," Krouch exclaimed half angrily. "Let's get this conversation started."

Nogales said slowly and impressively,

"Krouch, I've got ways of learning things that I'm not ready to tell you about right away." Again the hesitation, then Nogales continued, picking his words carefully as if not exactly trusting Krouch, as if fearful of saying too much, "There's one thing you'll have to answer me first — that is: would you be willing to put a little money into a proposition if you could pull out more than you put in?"

Krouch eyed Nogales sharply. "I'm doing that all the time," he replied suspiciously. "It all depends on the proposition."

Nogales poured two drinks from the bottle standing on the table, rolled and lighted a cigarette while Krouch squirmed with impatience. The two men drank again. Nogales settled himself comfortably. "Tanner, as you probably know," he began, "is tied up on a deal with the Southwest Cattle Company."

"That's common knowledge," Krouch snapped.

Nogales nodded. "I reckon so. Anyway, that means that he is in a position to keep the Southwest Cattle Company informed on what takes place around these parts. Am I right?"

"I suppose so," Krouch conceded cautiously. "Go on."

"Suppose," Nogales said softly, "that Tanner wanted to get hold of Lena Lou's Star-M Ranch but didn't have enough money to swing the deal. The next thing he'd do would be to try and get the Southwest Cattle Company interested, wouldn't he?"

"Sounds plausible." Krouch nodded. "He'd probably try, anyway. But I don't know what good it would do him. If the Southwest Cattle Company had wanted the Star-M, they'd have gone after it long ago. That company is a right wealthy organization."

"True." Nogales nodded. "We'll say you're right when you state that if the company had wanted the Star-M it would have bought the ranch long ago. Maybe it didn't want it then. But suppose — just suppose — conditions have changed, and that now the Southwest Company suddenly wants the property. That makes the Star-M look like a good buy, doesn't it, if somebody can get in ahead of the Southwest Cattle Company?"

"Say, Scott — Anderson — whatever your name is — what in hell are you driving at?" Krouch demanded.

"This." Nogales' voice raised a trifle. "I've worked hard in my time and I haven't spent everything I've earned. I can still raise some money — say around twenty thousand dollars — if I see something good to invest it in —"

"Huh!" Krouch stared. "I thought you just told me you were shy on cash."

"Ready cash," Nogales said promptly. "I can't spend the twenty thousand right to once. I've got to be careful for a spell. Did you ever hear of marked bills?"

Krouch guffawed. "Then you didn't make that twenty thousand punching cows? And so the Otera Savings Bank marks its bills —"

"Forget that," Nogales said angrily. "It's none of your business where I get my *dinero*." Then he relaxed. "Hell, there's no use us going on the prod against each other. Let's talk sense."

"What's your proposition?" Krouch growled.

"Here it is: I'll put in my twenty thousand, if you'll add fifteen thousand to it, and we'll buy the Star-M. Then, when the Southwest Cattle Company comes after it, they'll have to pay our price. And they'll be dealing with two men instead of a girl who doesn't know anything about business."

Krouch was staring at Nogales, open-mouthed, wide-eyed. He seemed unable to find his voice. His mouth kept opening and closing without sound, like a fish out of water, gasping for air.

Nogales said, "Well, what do you say?"

Krouch's reply came with an explosive rush: "What! Are you insane? Thirty-five thousand for the Star-M! Maybe you're crazy — I'm sure you are! — but don't get the idea I'm crazy, too."

Nogales smiled confidently. "Sure, I'm crazy — like a wise old owl! On the surface of things thirty-five thousand dollars looks like a mighty big price for the Star-M Ranch in its present condition, run down like it is —"

"It's a crazy, insane, unheard-of price! It's — it's —" The sputtering, amazed Krouch ran out of words.

"Now wait a minute," Nogales said. "Suppose we do a mite of thinking on the proposition —"

"I refuse to give such an idiotic suggestion a thought," Krouch stormed.

"All right." Nogales shrugged careless shoulders. "I'll just have to raise all the money by myself —"

"In its present run-down condition," Krouch snapped, "nobody but a fool would pay thirty-five thousand for the Star-M!"

"Even a fool might," Nogales drawled, "*if* — and I'll do some more supposing or whatever you want to call it — *if there was oil on that land.*" He settled back to let the words sink in.

Came a sudden scraping of chair legs as Krouch half leaped from his chair and leaned across the table, staring into Nogales' amused eyes. The light of amazement slowly changed in Krouch's features to one of pure avariciousness.

"Oil!" Krouch yelled. "Oil?"

"Calm down," Nogales laughed. "There's no use of you telling the world."

"Calm down!" Krouch said indignantly. "You tell me there's oil on the Star-M and you expect me to be calm about it?"

"I still don't see any use of spreading the news all over Orejano. Somebody else might have the money to buy the place. If you're not interested just say so, and I'll raise the money some place else —"

"Who says I'm not interested?" Krouch exclaimed, then grew cautious again. "How do you know there's oil on the Star-M holdings?"

Nogales pretended impatience. "Good Lord, man! Do you have to see it gushing out of the ground before you'll believe it? Oh, shucks, I'm wasting time with you." Pretending sudden anger, Nogales rose from his chair. "Krouch, I've said all I intend to say. I don't know anything about you, and you might double-cross me. I've made you an offer. If you don't want to go in with me, why I'll —"

Krouch grabbed at his sleeve and forced him back into his chair, then again sat down. Beads of perspiration stood out on his forehead. His eyes sparkled greedily. "Wait! Wait!" he implored. "Give me a chance. Have they had some oil sharps looking into the proposition?" he asked hoarsely.

There was the light of truth in Nogales' eyes as he replied, "Frankly, I couldn't say. Remember, I only got here a few days back. I can't learn all the details in that short time."

Krouch gazed steadily at Nogales and saw the light of frankness in Nogales' gray eyes which didn't waver under the other man's steady, intense scrutiny. "Does Lena Lou know there's oil there?" he snapped finally.

Nogales laughed scornfully. "If you told that girl there was oil on her Star-M, she'd think you were plumb crazy," he replied. "Furthermore, if she knew there was oil on her land, you'd never get her place for a measly thirty-five thousand." Something of irritation crept into Nogales' tone now. "Krouch, I've told you my proposition. I'm offering to put in more than you. I'll have my twenty thousand ready when you produce fifteen grand. But if you're going in this with me, we've got to work fast. Are you coming in — or are you afraid to take a chance?"

"Wait — wait a minute!" Krouch was nervous, a trifle frantic, his mind already making plans. He waved one detaining hand as Nogales again made as if to rise from his chair. "Just sit still a minute. I've got to think this out."

Nogales, sure that his fish was hooked, sat back to wait, a frowning, impatient, irritated expression on his features. Krouch eyed him uneasily. Right now Krouch was more than half convinced there was oil on Lena Lou's land. The very fact that Nogales was willing to put in twenty thousand dollars against his own fifteen thousand was sufficient proof for

Krouch. Straub Krouch considered himself a shrewd judge of character; he hadn't been able to detect any lies in Nogales' statements.

Krouch was more concerned with another thought: why shouldn't he pretend to go in with Nogales but instead buy the Star-M for himself alone, without taking the cowboy in on the deal? In that way there'd be no pardner to divide profits with. That was an idea! Afterward, when Nogales learned he'd been swindled, if he got nasty, Krouch could simply tip off the law authorities as to the whereabouts of one Red Anderson. And there'd be a fifteen-hundred-dollar reward for that little action, too. Krouch licked his lips. Things were certainly breaking his way. As the plan took complete form in his mind the crook became all a-tremble in his cupidity.

Nogales, across the table, watched Krouch closely and made a good guess as to the thoughts passing through the man's mind. "There's one thing I forgot to tell you, Krouch," he said softly.

"What's that?"

"There was a representative of the Southwest Cattle Company at the Star-M this morning to talk to Lena Lou. He asked her if she'd take thirty thousand for her place?"

"My Gawd!" Krouch straightened in his chair. "Why didn't you tell me this before? She didn't close the deal, did she?"

"I happen to know she didn't," Nogales said. "Maybe she wanted time to think things over. That will never do. If she thinks too long she'll boost her price sky-high, whether she knows anything or not. That's why I suggested that we offer her thirty-five thousand for her place. I knew we'd have to raise the ante if we wanted to do business with her."

That settled it in Straub Krouch's mind. If the Southwest Cattle Company was willing to pay thirty thousand for the Star-M, it must be worth more. There was something behind all this, all right. If the company wanted the ranch, Krouch wanted it worse. Of that he was firmly convinced now. He leaped suddenly from his chair. "Good Gawd! I wish you'd told me all this before. You've wasted valuable time. Who is this cattle company representative? Has he been in town? Where can —"

Nogales said disgustedly, "*I'm* wasting valuable time? You got your nerve, you have, making a crack about me wasting time. All you've done is talk. Hell! I'm sick of fooling around you. I'm going to get some action or know the reason why." He rose suddenly from his chair and started for the doorway, speaking over his shoulder: "S'long, I'm heading to find some other capital to interest in this proposition —"

Krouch, his face flushed with excitement, leaped after Nogales. "Don't leave, don't

229

leave," he begged excitedly. "You and I can work this thing out together. It's just that I haven't much money on hand right now."

Nogales paused, hard-faced. "Can you raise it or can't you?" he demanded.

Krouch nodded. "Yes, I can make the grade with what I've got in the bank at Arroyo City. I'll have to go there to get it. At the same time I'll slap a mortgage on the Circle-Slash. . . . I'll raise the money, don't worry."

Nogales nodded. "Good. When will you want my twenty thousand?"

"We'll settle that later," Krouch said swiftly. "I'll raise the whole amount while I'm at it, then you can pay me after the deal is closed."

Nogales smiled inwardly, realizing what Krouch contemplated doing. "All right," he replied, "I'll have the money ready when you ask for it. Right now, before you go to Arroyo City, you'd better ride right out to the Star-M and see Lena Lou before that Southwest Cattle Company representative talks to her again. Get an option on the land. We can't waste time, you know."

"Good idea! I'll do it!" Krouch panted in his excitement.

"Don't mention that I'm with you on the proposition," Nogales advised, "and above all don't say a word about oil."

Krouch laughed triumphantly. "Do you think I'm crazy?"

With that he plunged through the doorway to the street, nearly knocking over Mike Artora, who was standing on the Apache porch, in his haste. Reaching his pony, he climbed quickly into the saddle and started plying his quirt and spurs at the same time. His pony leaped down the street in long strides and in a few minutes had disappeared from view.

Nogales stood looking after him, his eyes smiling. He mused, "Maybe you're not crazy, Krouch, but you're sure insane to get your hands on money that doesn't belong to you. That flaw in your make-up is what upsets your thinking apparatus." He turned to Mike Artora, who was still gazing in open-mouthed astonishment after his boss. "Mike, Krouch has right good taste in liquor. I reckon I'll go back and sample some more of his private stock, while I wait for his return."

"The boss, he come back soon — no?" Mike asked.

"He come back — yes," Nogales grinned. Then, noticing the small Mexican boy still holding his pony in the roadway, Nogales tossed the youngster a silver dollar. "That's all, *amigo. Muchas gracias.* I won't be leaving soon. Just move that bronc over to the hitch rack and tie him up. I'm staying here until something definite happens."

19. Lena Lou Runs a Bluff

Straub Krouch's pony was in a lather of sweat and blood by the time it reached the Star-M Ranch. The horse's hide had been slashed cruelly by Krouch's metal-tipped quirt, and its head drooped when Krouch, sawing impatiently on the spade bit, jerked the pony back to haunches in the Star-M ranch yard, a few yards distant from Lena Lou's back door.

Lena Lou had heard the pounding of approaching hoofs and had rushed to her doorway to see who was arriving at such a furious gait. A look of disgust swept across her features as she viewed the horse and rider.

"Straub Krouch," she cried, "the last time you were here I warned you not to come again." She reached just inside the doorway where her six-shooter hung on the wall in its holster. "Have I got to unravel a flock of lead in your direction to make you understand I wasn't talking just to hear myself?"

"Now put that gun back," Krouch panted, slipping from his saddle and coming toward her. "I've got important business with you."

"Not with me, you haven't," Lena Lou said

firmly. The gun tilted a trifle. "On your way, mister!"

"But, look here, Lena Lou," the man persisted, coming to a stop, "I want to talk serious. . . . I'm aiming to buy the Star-M —"

"Oh pshaw!" the girl countered contemptuously. "That again? I thought we'd settled that before. I'm not interested in your offers until you can show me some real money. Five thousand won't touch this outfit —"

"I know, I know I haven't offered enough," Krouch said contritely. "Five thousand is small money. I'm willing to raise the ante. I'll give you ten thousand —"

"On your way!" Lena Lou half turned away though she still kept the gun level in Krouch's direction. "Get going!"

"Fifteen thousand!" Krouch raised his voice.

Lena Lou swung back toward the man. "I don't want to have to warn you again," she said softly, but her eyes were cold. "This gun of mine is in good working order, Krouch. I just cleaned and oiled it this morning. Lots of oil makes the mechanism work mighty smoothly. Do I have to prove that to you?"

Krouch stared at her, his mouth falling open. What did she mean by that word 'oil'? Was there a hidden meaning there? Maybe this girl was wiser than he had considered her. He decided to take a chance on her pulling trigger. "Listen, Lena Lou," he commenced earnestly, "I want you to under-stand —"

"*Miss Morley* to you, Krouch," the girl broke in.

"All right then," Krouch stammered, flus-tered. "Listen, Miss Morley, listen to reason. I'm talking business. I'm not asking you again to marry me —"

"That's a relief," Lena Lou said dryly.

"— I'm here on strict business. I'll prove it to you. I'm willing to pay you twenty thou-sand dollars for your outfit! That's my last word on the subject. Take it or leave it."

Lena Lou half lowered her gun and looked sharply at the man. There must be some new reason on Krouch's part to account for this sudden decision to boost his offer for the Star-M. Then the girl remembered Nogales' words earlier in the day. Lena Lou liked and trusted Nogales; maybe his hand was in this offer of Krouch's. What was it Nogales had told her? Oh yes . . .

Lena Lou smiled suddenly. She'd back Nogales' play even if she didn't understand what it was all about. "*Mister Krouch*," she in-formed him sweetly, "you'll have to boost the ante some more if you expect to do business with me."

"I've given you my highest figure," Krouch said stiffly. Lena Lou shrugged slim shoul-ders. "Suit yourself. However, you may be in-terested to know I was talking to a gentleman this morning who asked me if I'd take *thirty thousand* for my outfit."

Krouch staggered a little. This was almost a deathblow. It was all true then. She had been offered thirty thousand! Beads of perspiration stood out on Krouch's forehead. He was growing desperate.

"Th— th— thirty thousand?" he gasped.

"Thirty thousand, Krouch." Lena Lou smiled, enjoying his discomfiture. "So you'll have to crawl up out of the ditch if you expect to do business with me."

The girl didn't understand what it was all about but, sensing her advantage, she decided to press it to the full. She laughed contemptuously and turned back into the house. Shoving her gun back in holster, she said coldly, "And I'm not at all certain I want to do business with you — now or any time. Good-by, Krouch." She nodded shortly and closed the door.

It was a strong bluff to make, but by this time Lena Lou was certain Krouch wouldn't leave. In this her intuition proved correct.

Krouch stared speechless for just one minute, then he made a wild leap for the porch and commenced pounding on the closed door.

Lena Lou opened up and stood facing him a moment. "No, thanks, nothing today," she said and started to close the door again.

"Wait, wait for Gawd's sake, Lena Lou —

Miss Morley," Krouch stammered. "You've got to give me some consideration —"

"Consideration?" Lena Lou eyed the man coldly.

"Look — look — Miss Morley" — shoving his foot between the door and the jamb to prevent the girl from closing the door in his face again — "I'll — I'll give you thirty-five thousand for the Star-M!"

Lena Lou's eyes widened a trifle. "Krouch!" she commenced, scarcely knowing what to say, her surprise was so great, "I —"

Krouch misinterpreted the look in her eyes. He thought she was holding out for a still higher figure. "All right, all right," he shouted, "I don't like to haggle, either. I'll raise it. Forty thousand it is! I won't go a cent higher."

Lena Lou suddenly felt weak all over. She couldn't hold out any longer. She opened the door wider. "All right, I'll take forty thousand," she said, "but you'll have to come across with the cash before I'll believe you. If you can't raise the money," she added, "somebody else can." And now she was bluffing again.

"Cash! Cash?" Krouch said. "I haven't forty thousand cash with me, naturally. I'll take an option with what money's in my pocket. I'll give you a check and notes for the balance tomorrow or next day."

Lena Lou interrupted, again remembering

Nogales' words: "I won't take notes, Krouch. I want cash, or the deal's off."

Krouch was inside the kitchen now. "Cash!" He stared at the girl. She was getting sharper all the time. By now Krouch was ready to find a hidden import in every word.

"Yes, cash," Lena Lou said decidedly. "If you don't want to do business on that basis, there's the door. Use it."

Krouch surrendered. "All right, I'll get cash for you," he announced. "How about a three-day option? It may take a little time to raise all cash money. I'll try to be here with the money tomorrow, but in case anything goes wrong, I'll need a little extra time. Three-day option, eh?"

Had Krouch asked for a thirty-day option, Lena Lou would have given the matter small thought, but when he spoke of a three-day option, she realized he was in great haste to get the matter settled.

Once more she pressed her advantage, shaking her head. "Nothing doing on a three-day option. I'll give you a two-day option — not a minute longer. Unless you arrive here with the money this very instant day after tomorrow, Straub Krouch, you lose out. Is that clear?"

Krouch stared at her, startled. He'd never thought this slip of a girl could grow so hard. "Look here, you're crowding me for time, Miss Morley —"

"Suit yourself." Lena Lou shrugged careless shoulders. "I didn't ask you to buy my place. I told you once to get out — more than once, I reckon. Even held a gun on you and you wouldn't take a hint. You practically forced your way into my kitchen. And now you're trying to dictate terms. You get funnier all the time. We'd better call the whole thing off. On your way, mister, I've wasted enough time —"

"Don't get me wrong, don't get me wrong," Krouch interrupted hastily. "It's all right with me. Sure, a two-day option is fine. Let's make out the paper now."

He thrust a shaking hand into one pocket and brought forth a handful of silver, gold and some soiled bills. "Let's see . . ." he muttered, starting to count the money and mentally damning his lack of foresight in not bringing more from the Apache when he left. Maybe the girl would refuse to take such a small amount. He finished counting and thrust the money toward Lena Lou.

"There you are. One hundred sixty-five dollars and forty-five cents. I reckon that covers the option money."

"Maybe," Lena Lou said coolly, sending more cold shivers down Krouch's spine. She counted the money carefully and when she had finished: "All right. Wait here while I go write out the paper."

Krouch heaved a long sigh of relief and

mopped his wet forehead as he dropped into a chair. Within a few minutes Lena Lou returned from another room with a paper, signed, covering the option, which she passed over to Krouch.

Krouch studied intently every written word. Yes, it was all there. "Maybe we should have this witnessed by a law sharp," he suggested.

At the moment Lena Lou spied old Pablo coming up from the corral. "Why do you want a lawyer?" she asked sharply. "It's all there in black and white. If you want a witness, we'll let Pablo do the witnessing. He knows *my* signature, and *you* know anything I sign is good. If that's not satisfactory, tear up the paper. Here, take your money."

Krouch shook his head, shunning the money as he might have the plague. There wasn't any further argument; he gave in once more. He wiped his forehead. This seemed to be his day to be rushed into things. Still feeling a trifle weak, he rose from the chair and, with the option, witnessed by old Pablo, in his pocket, walked shakily out to his horse and climbed into the saddle.

Lena Lou watched him turn the pony and head out toward the trail that left the house. Once he was out of sight, she sank limply into a chair. "Pablo," she said slowly, "I still don't know what this is all about, but it looks as though we've sold the Star-M for a heap more money than the old place is worth. If I didn't feel that Nogales was back of all this business I'd sure think something was mighty wrong. As it is I'm just thankful."

Old Pablo beamed toothily. "Maybe for the suppair tonight we have chicken — no?"

"Good grief, *yes*, Pablo!" She thrust some money into his hand. "And anything else you want!"

20. "Put Those Cows Through"

After leaving the Star-M, instead of heading directly back to Orejano, Straub Krouch cut across country until he struck a trail running to his own Circle-Slash outfit. Here he swung his horse about, heading for home and plying a vigorous quirt on his weary mount. He rode steadily, chuckling to himself at the manner in which he intended to cheat Red Anderson — or Nogales — out of his share of the profits to be made from a re-sale of the Star-M Ranch.

His horse was just rounding a clump of chaparral at a bend in the road when his ear caught the sound of a running horse. The next instant Krouch's foreman, Ward Austen, broke through some brush at the edge of the trail and reined in at Krouch's side.

Krouch lifted one hand in greeting. "It's lucky I met you, Austen," Krouch said, "it'll save me the rest of the trip home. Where you heading for?"

"I was just coming in to tell you," Austen laughed, "that you can come direct to the Phantom Pass house tonight. I reckon we're both saved a trip. We got the cows moved over there like you ordered. All the boys are there too, even the cook. I had him bring some supplies and come along, so the boys wouldn't have to return to the house for feeding. Me and Stan Cox had some words. With two broken arms he can't help none with the cows, so I told him to stay at the ranch and keep an eye on things. He wouldn't do it, though — said he didn't have to take orders from anybody but you. I think we should settle that matter, Straub, as to who's boss —"

"I'm boss," Krouch snapped. "Forget Cox. If you can't handle my crew, I'll get somebody who can."

"I'm sorry," Austen said sulkily. "But, you see —"

"Did you start fixing over those brands?" Krouch broke in.

Austen shook his head. "That was something else I wanted to see you about. You said something yesterday about not waiting to re-brand but you didn't finish what you were saying. I wasn't sure —"

"We won't bother re-branding this time," Krouch said. "I want those cows put through that pass tonight, Austen. I'm afraid that rifle shot the other night has busted up our ghost scheme. Whoever fired that shot knows those ghosts aren't genuine."

"Cripes! I wouldn't worry none about that if I was you, Straub. You haven't heard anything more about it. That shot was probably fired by somebody just passing through the country. I didn't think so at first, but since nothing has happened since, I've made up my mind to forget it —"

"Nothing happened, eh?" Krouch growled. "Except we've lost four men — Ronson, Webster, Furlow and the Nevada Kid —"

"You know who was responsible for that. You can't connect those two cowpokes with that rifle shot at the ghost herd."

"I won't connect one of 'em," Krouch grunted, "but I'm not so sure about the other. Somebody in this country is bucking us. Things haven't been going so well of late —"

"Ah, that's just the breaks of the game, boss. Call it luck — bad luck, if you like, but that will change —"

"I'm not tempting bad luck too far nor waiting for it to change, either, Austen. You put those cows through the pass tonight. Get 'em delivered to that cowman across the line and tell him to change his own brands this time, if he wants 'em changed. Get cash money from him. Tell him there won't be any more stock comin' through for a spell, as I'm figuring on laying low, as regards rustling, for a while until things calm down. Later, we can resume business as usual."

"Aren't you going to be on hand to run the business tonight?" Austen asked, with some surprise.

Krouch shook his head. "You'll have to handle it, Austen. I've got to leave for Arroyo City tonight to raise some money. I'll probably be back tomorrow. I've got a good thing on this time, Austen — big profits —" He paused. "Did you ever hear of an outlaw named Red Anderson?"

Austen pondered the question a moment. "Red Anderson? Sounds sort of familiar. He ain't the feller that robbed the bank and killed the sheriff over Otera way, is he?"

"That's the hombre. Right now he's living under the name of Nogales Scott —"

"Nogales Scott!" Austen's eyes widened. "Well, I'll be damned! How did you find him out?"

"I've got ways of learning things," Krouch said importantly.

"I'll bet you have," Austen flattered. "Folks don't put much over on you. How about that Caliper hombre — Nogales' pardner? Is he riding the owl-hoot trail too?"

Krouch shook his head. "I don't think so. He's one of these goody-goody hombres. Nogales — or Anderson — and Caliper had an argument and split up. I've got a hunch Caliper learned who Nogales was, and it didn't set right, but being Nogales was once a pard, Caliper is keeping his mouth shut. . . . There's a fifteen-hundred reward on Red Anderson's head."

"There is?" Austen looked interested. "Why

don't you turn him in and collect?"

Krouch laughed slyly. "Exactly what I intend to do later. I've got to pretend to be friendly to him for a few days, though, or else he'll spoil a scheme I'm working on. He thinks by putting some money in with me, he'll be in on the profits, but I'm not going to take his money until I got things sewed up in my own name. Then I'll take his money and — well, it wouldn't look right for me to turn a pardner over to the authorities, so I reckon I'll just let you and the boys turn his scalp over to the authorities and collect the reward. That'll make a nice bonus for you."

Austen grinned admiringly. "You always were a smart one, chief. Your brain works every minute. No wonder you get along like you do."

The two men talked a few minutes longer, then parted, Austen heading back toward Phantom Pass, while Krouch turned his pony in the direction of Orejano.

The sun was low when Krouch arrived in town. He had pushed his pony hard every inch of the way, and when he slid from the saddle before the Apache Saloon tie rail, the pony nearly dropped. Krouch gave the poor beast a final slash across the head with his quirt, muttered something about "lousy horseflesh" and went on toward the saloon entrance.

Nogales was still waiting when Krouch entered. The wait had been tiresome, but now that the whole town took him for Red Anderson, Nogales figured he'd better not stir out, for fear some intrepid soul might try to collect a reward. He'd found some old newspapers to read, and the contents of the Old Crow bottle was lowered an inch or more, so the time spent in waiting hadn't been entirely wasted.

"Well, it took you long enough," Nogales grumbled as Krouch dropped into a chair across the table. He suspected that Krouch had covered other ground than that which had taken him to the Star-M.

"Couldn't be helped," Krouch grunted, wiping the sweat from his forehead. "That gang bronc of mine's got sleeping sickness or somethin'. Couldn't get any speed out of him a-tall. Cripes, I'm dry!" He seized the bottle and poured himself a good two fingers of bourbon, swallowed it and went on: "I rode fast as I could both ways. I had to talk harder'n I ever did before in my life —"

"The main thing is," Nogales interrupted impatiently, "did you get an option on the Star-M?"

"That's what I went after, isn't it? Sure I got it. Straub Krouch gets what he goes after every time. I — we had to pay her more'n we figured on, though. That dang gal held me up for forty thousand. . . . Insisted on cash too. I tell you, she knows something is afoot —"

246

"That's probable." Nogales nodded, inwardly rejoicing. Lena Lou was a pretty smart girl. He continued, "But she doesn't know everything Krouch, not by a long shot. Forty thousand, eh? Well, that looks like we'd both be putting up twenty thousand now instead of you just putting up fifteen thousand like we planned. Oh well, that will make it more equal."

"It may make it more equal," Krouch said disgruntledly, "but it means I'll have to put a mortgage on the Apache as well as on the Circle-Slash, I'm afraid —"

"When do we get the deed?" Nogales asked.

"Lena Lou will have the deed and so on all ready when I show up with the money. Once I get her bill of sale, the legal aspects, transferring title and that stuff, can be taken care of later."

Nogales nodded. "How come she jacked you up to forty thousand dollars?" he asked. "There hasn't been a Southwest Cattle Company representative after her again, has there?"

"I don't know." Krouch shook his head. "Something got into that gal. She acted like she was doing me a favor when she sold me the place. Independent as a hawg on ice, she was. She must have heard a hint drop some place that the value of her place would be increased or something of the kind. I figure we are lucky getting her place now."

"I wouldn't be surprised," Nogales agreed. "At that, the price is reasonable, I figure, knowing what I know. When do you want my twenty thousand?"

"No rush about that," Krouch said hurriedly. "We'll get the papers for the property all squared away first, then you can give me your money." He showed the option to Nogales, then rose to his feet. "I've been figuring right along on taking a train that comes through here about nine o'clock tonight but I just happened to think there's a freight through here in about half an hour. I aim to flag that and ride to Arroyo City in the caboose. Maybe I can see Banker Jarvis tonight and have everything arranged to get the money in the morning —"

"You sure he'll let you have the money?"

"He never refused me yet. I've got some notes there now but I've kept up the interest, and he's always been willing to lend. And with the Apache and Circle-Slash as security, he wouldn't run any risk on the loan. By train it's not much of a run to Arroyo City, so I figure I'll be back by tomorrow afternoon, if nothing happens."

"Don't you let anything happen," Nogales warned sternly. "You stay right on the job until you've taken up that option and got Lena Lou's bill of sale. Options have been known to be proved worthless — when more money is offered. I don't aim to let this deal slip through my fingers. If it does, it's your fault. Then — well, look out for me, that's all!"

Nogales patted his holster meaningly as the final words left his lips.

Krouch himself was no mean hand with a six-shooter but he read a menace in Nogales' eyes that couldn't be ignored. "Don't you worry," he laughed a bit nervously. "I'll put this deal through, all right."

"See that you do," Nogales said coldly.

He followed Krouch to the door and watched the man cross the street and pass between two buildings, on his way to the tiny 'dobe railroad station at which trains seldom stopped. Far in the distance a train whistle sounded faintly.

"I reckon he's on his way," Nogales laughed shortly. He strode out to the hitch rail, mounted his pony and started it at a swift lope in the direction of the Maple-Leaf Ranch.

So far things appeared to be working out satisfactorily.

21. Caliper's Discovery

It was dark when Nogales rode into the Maple-Leaf ranch yard. As he neared the corral he noticed a number of horses, saddled up and waiting. "I reckon I've been detaining the boys," he told himself.

From the lighted bunkhouse came the sounds of voices. He bent his steps in that direction.

"Here's the old snail hoof at last," Caliper greeted as Nogales entered. "Just like a cow's tail — you're always behind!"

"And you're just like a pack mule," Nogales retorted, "— always kicking!" He glanced around at Tanner and the other waiting punchers. "I'm plumb sorry to have kept you waiting, rannies," he continued, "but it couldn't be helped. I've been helping Lena Lou put through a deal for her Star-M."

"You have?" Tanner exclaimed. "Who's buying?"

"Straub Krouch. Paying right good money, too, considering the way the Star-M's run down. Forty thousand dollars."

"What? Forty thousand dollars!" repeated an incredulous chorus of voices. The men stared at Nogales in blank amazement.

Caliper pushed up to his pardner and sniffed at him, then turned to the others, shaking his head. "Nope, Nogales isn't drunk, though I do detect a faint aroma of bourbon — very excellent bourbon. Tell us about it, Nogales."

"I'll give you the details when we get more time," Nogales replied. "We've got to get riding to Phantom Pass right soon. To cut the story short Krouch has an idea the Southwest Cattle Company is trying to buy the Star-M. He was out to the Star-M this afternoon and got an option from Lena Lou. She gets the money tomorrow, if nothing goes wrong —"

"But *forty thousand* dollars," Tanner said, shaking his head. "In its present condition — and Krouch should be informed on the facts — it's not worth that much money."

"It is," Nogales contradicted, grinning, "if it's got oil on it."

"Oil!" Tanner exclaimed scornfully. "There's no oil within a hundred miles of here —"

Nogales drawled, "That may be so — but you can't get Krouch to believe it."

Gradually it dawned on Caliper what Nogales had done. The other men stood about with open mouths, unbelieving, while Caliper laughed gleefully. "Nogales, you lying old catfish! Did you tell Krouch there was oil to be found on the Star-M? Aren't you ashamed — trifling with the truth thataway?"

"Who, me?" Nogales assumed an air of injured innocence. "You don't think *I'd* tell a lie, do you, Caliper?" He could keep his face straight no longer. "Nope, I didn't tell a lie. I didn't have to. Fact is I didn't make any definite statements that weren't true and couldn't be backed up. I just threw out a few *hints* and several *supposes*, and Krouch's imagination did the rest. He just leaped to his own conclusions. Last I saw of him he was heading for Arroyo City to get money to close the deal. He was so excited he was between a fit and a sweat."

The punchers were all laughing heartily, their eyes shining with admiration for Nogales. Only Caliper was puzzled now over a question that hadn't, apparently, occurred to the others.

"Look here, pard," Caliper frowned, "how come you got so thick with Krouch all of a sudden? I don't just understand him trusting you."

"Krouch thinks I'm a crook — just like he is. He got a fool idea into his head that I'm one Red Anderson who is wanted for murder and bank robbery. I happen to know that Red Anderson was captured and hung a spell back — but Krouch doesn't know that. I even had a hard time convincing Deputy Sheriff Burgett that I wasn't Anderson, until I pointed out to him the description on the reward bill that states Anderson had two fingers missing on his left hand."

"You're getting ahead of the story as far as I'm concerned," Tanner frowned. "Where does Burgett come in?"

Nogales gave terse details of his visit to the deputy sheriff's office, then went on: "Well, after I got Burgett to see the light and had explained conditions hereabouts, Burgett and I staged a fake fight. We both threw a lot of useless lead around, and I came tearing out of his office, forked my bronc and lit a shuck out of town. A little later Burgett gets on his bronc and hits out for my trail. He's due here at the Maple-Leaf later tonight. You see, he did me a favor, and now I figure to do him one."

Caliper looked blank. "Elucidate, cowboy, elucidate. What's the idea in all this?"

Nogales looked exasperatedly at his partner. "Caliper," he asked witheringly, "do you know the national song of Siam?"

"Do I what? Say, what you talking about? No, I don't know the national song of Siam."

"You'd better learn it then. It starts out on the first line with 'Oh, what an ass I am!' And the same words go for all the other lines. All you have to do is repeat it over and over. Being dumb, you're already qualified to sing it. Now listen close — in the first place Burgett and I put on that fake fight to impress Krouch with the fact I'm an outlaw with a price on my head. That was the favor he did me. Is that clear?"

"Fairly clear, coming from you," Caliper said sarcastically.

"Next," Nogales continued, "the reward bill for Red Anderson slipped out of my hand. Krouch picked it up and read it. That — coupled with the fight I'd had with Burgett — convinced Krouch I was not only a crook but one *hombre muy malo* — in short: a mighty tough customer. . . . Are you still with me, Caliper?"

"I'm commencing to gain on you," Caliper chuckled.

"All right," Nogales grinned. "I didn't want to leave you too far behind. . . . Now here's the favor I do Deputy Sheriff Burgett. He really would like to make good on his job but he's got a feeling that he was just stuck in there by a political ring as a figurehead. He'd like to surprise 'em. Tonight we go after the Phantom Pass rustlers. If we capture them we'll turn 'em over to Burgett and let him get the credit for a neat piece of work. That will build him up in the county. Now do you understand the plan?"

"I'd have understood it in the first place," Caliper growled, "if you didn't mumble your words so. Sure, the idea is fine; I've got a hunch it may work out, even if *you* did plan it. . . . And I'm not so dumb as you think I am, either. I've been mighty busy myself today."

"What have you been doing," Nogales queried sarcastically, "taking a bath?"

Caliper overlooked the insult in his eagerness to tell his story. "I've been thinking a lot about that country around Phantom Pass — wanted to look it over in daylight. I figured we should know the lay of the land if we're planning a night attack there. Well, Bud Thompson agreed with me, so we thought we'd take a ride over that way just to pass the time. Well, on the way we passed Krouch's Circle-Slash outfit —"

"You should have dropped in and made a friendly visit," Nogales chuckled.

"Quit interrupting me," Caliper snapped. "The rest of the boys have heard this story; I'm just repeating it for your benefit."

"I didn't know anybody was staging a benefit for me —"

"If you don't keep your trap closed, somebody will have to stage one for you to raise money for a hospital bill. . . . Anyway, the Circle-Slash buildings looked plumb deserted. Bud, being inquisitive, suggests that we drop in and get a drink of water just to see if the place really is deserted. As a matter of fact there wasn't a soul around the place. Not even a cook there —"

"I hope you snooped around some," Nogales said, interested.

"We not only snooped — we found something. In one barn we found a white horse and a bunch of cows. *Every one of those cows had been whitewashed —"*

"The ghost herd!" Nogales exclaimed. "That for certain, fastens the rustling, around here on Straub Krouch. Now we know what we've been suspecting."

Caliper nodded. "Yep, the ghost herd! The cows and that white horse all had streaks of black paint running crisscross and every other way on their hides —"

"What's the idea in that?" Nogales asked blankly.

"Don't you see," Caliper said, "those black streaks looked like branches and brush at a distance under moonlight? That's why we thought we were looking right through those ghosts the other night. With the moon clouded part of the time like it was, we were easily fooled, Nogales."

Nogales nodded. "It's a clever stunt, all right."

"Just an optical illusion like you said in the first place, pard. And we found a white canvas suit there for the ghost of Constado to wear. That was marked up with black streaks, too."

"Even white boots and a white sombrero," Bud Thompson put in. "And a white saddle — gosh, they didn't overlook a thing when they put on that act."

"Except," Nogales pointed out, "that it's dang hard to fool men with brains very long. Cripes, rannies! It looks like you've cleared up the mystery — all except how that ghost parade disappeared right before our very face and eyes."

"Don't crowd me and I'll do my work better," Caliper grinned. "Bud and I wondered about that, too, so, after leaving the Circle-Slash — and we wiped out all sign of our being there, first — we took a *pasear* over toward Phantom Pass. We didn't want to take a chance on being seen, so we circled wide and got up in the hills, where we could look right down on that old 'dobe house. Shucks! It was a cinch to work that disappearing act."

"Well, tell it, tell it!" Nogales urged.

"About fifty yards from the house," Caliper continued, "there's a ridge, covered with brush, not much higher than a rider's head so it's not very noticeable. All the ghosts had to do was parade along from behind the 'dobe house until they came to the ridge. When the ridge was reached they'd pass from view behind it —"

"Judas priest!" Nogales exclaimed.

Caliper went on: "Back of the ridge and running parallel with it is a long narrow hollow — sort of an arroyo — that extends in back of the house, too. After passing behind the ridge, the ghost parade dipped down into the hollow and followed it back to the house. Once the ghosts were behind the house they'd climb out of the hollow, come around the corner of the house and stage another parade —"

"Damn' if I don't believe you've hit it, Caliper — you and Bud," Nogales burst out. "Good work, cow-willies. Yep, that's the solution, all right. . . . Did you see anybody in the vicinity of Phantom Pass or the 'dobe house?"

"We sure did." Caliper nodded. "Our spying-out spot up in the hills was too far away for us to distinguish who they were, but there were five or six fellers there — maybe more — moving around. In that hollow back of the house a couple of riders were holding a bunch of cows, too —"

"There's our meat," Nogales said. "C'mon, let's get started. I've held you fellows up enough now."

"We're not in too much of a hurry for you to grab some chow first," Tanner suggested. "I've had Ting Low warming up your supper, while you talked. It's on the table by this time."

"If you can wait, I can." Nogales nodded. "I just remembered I haven't grubbed since breakfast." He started toward the doorway, on his way to the cook shanty then paused, asking, "How about me having a fresh horse, Lee? Can you fix me up? I've been working my bronc right hard the last couple of days, and while I'm eating I'd appreciate it if you'd feed and water him —"

"I'll take that chore, cowpoke," Caliper spoke up.

"Sure you can have a fresh horse, Nogales," Tanner spoke. "I don't know of anything around here you can't have —"

Caliper cut in, "I'll take on the job of roping him out a fresh pony, Lee," and he added maliciously, his eyes twinkling, "and I'll have a lot of fun picking a bronc that will spill him the first jump, too."

"You do," Nogales threatened, "and I'll tear off your ropin' arm and beat you over the head with it." Laughingly he passed through the doorway, headed for the cookhouse.

Twenty minutes later the cavalcade of eight men spurred their horses through the wide gate that fronted the Maple-Leaf ranch house and headed off across the range in the direction of Phantom Pass. Tanner, Nogales and Caliper led the procession, with the others strung out behind and fanning out a bit to avoid the dust kicked up by the flying hoofs of the leaders.

22. The Fight at the Pass!

About an hour later the Maple-Leaf horses pounded past Krouch's Circle-Slash buildings. All was quite dark; it was evident no one was there. On the riders went, the miles unrolling beneath the swift-moving hoofs of the speeding ponies. The faces of Tanner and his men were grim; for all the concern shown by Caliper's and Nogales' manner one might have thought they were on pleasure bent.

The sky along the horizon was commencing to lighten when the hogback near Phantom Pass was reached. In another fifteen minutes the moon would be up.

Instead of dismounting at the bottom of the hogback, the riders circled wide to reach one end. Here the horses were tethered in a thick jungle of manzanita, cacti, mesquite, sage and other growths familiar to the southwest country. So well were both men and animals screened by the brush that a stranger, passing by, would never have suspected their presence.

"You can't tell who might be prowling around," Tanner said. "We'll wait here until one of us can look over the situation."

"I'll climb up to the top of the hogback,"

260

Nogales proposed. "Caliper and I were up there the other night so we know the lay of the land. I'll get word to you if anything happens. If you don't hear from me right off, wait as patiently as you can. Sometime to-night we'll see action. I feel that in my bones."

"I'll go with you," Caliper offered.

"Come on."

Together the two cowboys left their companions and scrambled up the steeply sloping side of the high hog-back. Reaching the top, they at once threw themselves flat.

"Geez! Some climb!" Caliper panted, sprawling prone on the earth, with low brush growing around him.

"That so?" Nogales grinned. "I didn't think it was very far to the bottom, judging how quick you got down the other night when we were up here."

They focused eyes across the long stretch of land below them, to where Phantom Pass opened, grim and foreboding, between two pigged spires of rock. Not far from the pass two small squares of yellow light showed in one wall of the old adobe house.

"Somebody there," Nogales said. It wasn't necessary to whisper; they were too far away for their voices to carry to the house on which their gaze was fixed.

The scene commenced to brighten as the moon lifted above a jagged, mountainous ridge, far to their right. For some time the cowboys strained their eyes without seeing anybody. Then, as the moon mounted higher in the sky, shedding her silvery radiance over the surrounding country, several men emerged from the door of the adobe house and made their way around to the rear of the building. Some minutes passed, then to the two ear-straining cowboys came a faint, far-off bawling of cattle.

"I don't remember those cows in the ghost herd bellowing." Caliper mused. "It must be they muzzle 'em or something."

Nogales nodded, lost in thought. Nothing more was heard for some time. After awhile occasional sounds of cattle reached them.

Caliper shifted about impatiently. "I wish those scuts would get started, so we could get into action. Why can't we jump 'em now before they leave?"

Nogales shook his head. "There'd be too much chance for one or two of 'em to escape. If we wait until they get into the pass we'll have them practically cornered. The cows will be filling the pass in front; we'll come spurring in from the rear. In that way we should be able to account for every rustler in the bunch."

Again Nogales withdrew into silence, occupied with his own thoughts. His eyes were fixed on the adobe house, but his mind was many miles away.

"Hey! What you thinking about, pard?" Caliper grunted suddenly.

"Huh! What?" Absent-mindedly Nogales turned a bewildered, faraway gaze on his companion.

"What are you thinking about? You're so quiet —"

"Oh," Nogales sighed, roused himself, muttered something that had to do with settling down and raising poultry.

Caliper's jaw dropped. "Write poetry?" he said in amazement.

"No, nitwit, not write poetry — raise poultry."

Caliper's brow cleared, "Oh, I thought you said *poetry*. I was wondering if you were going to have another of those lit'ry streaks, like that time you read a book and took to composing epitaphs —"

"Not epitaphs, Caliper," Nogales said with some irritation, "epigrams."

"Well, epigrams then; I don't see what difference it makes. They both seem to be the final word on something."

Nogales smiled and pointed out the difference: "My epigrams I write with a lead pencil. My epitaphs are written with lead too, only it comes out of a six-shooter."

Caliper steered back to former channels of thought: "We're getting off the track. What's all that got to do with raising poultry? Where'd you get that idea?"

"What, raising poultry? Oh, I — well, you see, that chicken dinner we had at Lena Lou's the first night we were there sort of put it into my head, in a way. I got to thinking life would be plumb rosy if a feller could sit down to a meal like that every night. And if you could have that same good cooking for breakfast, too. . . ." Nogales' voice died off into silence.

"Yeah, that would be great, wouldn't it?" There was a long pause with no word spoken between the two men, then Caliper continued: "Say, have you been feeling that way too?"

"What way?" Nogales asked cautiously.

"Oh . . . er . . . no particular way . . . just sort of . . . sweet on her . . . y'know, you get a sort of empty feeling near the belt buckle every time Lena Lou smiles at you. Kind of as if you ought to change your shirt every day and shave reg'lar and . . . and . . ."

Nogales turned his face directly toward Caliper. "Yeah, I'm that way. I'm not denying it any. Caliper, old pard, we may have to split up our riding the trails together. It's all right for you, but it's time I was settled down. I'm going to ask Lena Lou to marry me. You know, Caliper, a man should have a regular home at my age and a couple of sons running around —" He broke off suddenly at the look in Caliper's face under the pale light of the moon. "Say, do you feel the same way, pard? Don't tell me you fell, too."

Caliper nodded dumbly. After a few moments he found his tongue: "I never suspected you were feeling the same way. It must be the weather or something. . . . Nogales, you and I never disagreed serious on anything yet. We're not going to commence now. I'll drop out. You can have Lena Lou. I'll keep still and let you do the talking —"

"No, no! You'll do nothing of the kind," Nogales replied, his voice miserable. "It'd probably be you she'd marry. You're a heap better looking than I am — better at riding and roping, too, not to mention bronc busting —"

"But you could always shoot rings around me —"

"I'll keep clear and not interfere, Caliper," Nogales said, martyred resignation in his tones.

"No siree! You can marry her, Nogales. We've been pards a lot of years now and I don't aim to spoil your happiness. You'll make Lena Lou a lot better husband than I —"

"You're all wrong, Caliper. You've got those tender ways that women like. I've watched you branding dogies and I could see it hurt you, the way you put the hot iron to their sides. That's what appeals to the feminine mind —"

"I know, I know," Caliper admitted his virtues, "but I've been a drinking man all my life —"

"So have I —"

And so they wrangled, while the minutes flew swiftly by, with still no sign of movement before the old adobe house. The moon climbed higher, while each man tried to persuade the other as to who should be the one to lead Lena Lou to the altar.

"I'll tell you what!" Nogales had been struck by a brilliant idea: "We'll both ask her together, and no matter which one she chooses, it won't make any difference to the other one. We'll go on being pards just the same —"

"We sure would. We couldn't let any woman come between us."

"— and if I win, you can live in the same house with us, and if she picks you, I'll live at your house."

Caliper nodded enthusiastically. "That's a right idea. Let's shake on it."

They shook hands with considerable solemnity.

Nogales said generously, "Go in and win, cowpoke. The best of luck to you."

"Same to you, pard."

"And don't forget, faint heart never won a bronc-peeling contest. Like I say, cowpoke, don't be bashful — go in to win." And then in a muttered undertone: "— if you can."

That settled it for a few minutes, until Caliper suddenly blurted out, "Say, y'know it won't be so bad at that — having you living at my house all the time. You'll be company for us."

"What d'you mean, living at *your* house?" Nogales demanded in some surprise. "Don't count your herd before it's branded, cowboy. As a matter of fact I was just wondering if Lena Lou would object to having a boarder at *my* house."

Caliper was about to reply when a movement down at the old adobe place caught his eye. "We'll settle it later, Nogales. There's the cows starting to move."

A herd of between thirty and fifty beef animals was just being driven around the corner of the old house and headed in the direction of Phantom Pass. One man led the herd, two flanked the sides and five more riders were strung out in the rear.

The next instant the two cowboys were sliding down the side of the hogback in a shower of dust and gravel. By the time they arrived at the spot where Tanner and his men were waiting, their horses were being held, ready for mounting.

Tanner and the others were already in saddle. "We heard you coming," Tanner said, as they came running up to the knot of riders. "It sounded as if you were bringing the whole hogback with you. Did you see anything?"

"Plenty," Nogales answered, vaulting into the saddle. "They've got the herd started and are heading toward Phantom Pass right now. They'll probably be inside before we get there. There's more 'n just your thirty blooded critters in the bunch. Maybe they've added some of the Star-M stock to their gathering —"

Tanner said, "The Star-M is already practically wiped out. It's more probable they picked up some of my cows from some place else."

"Regardless whether they're Maple-Leaf or what they are," Caliper cut in, "we've got to stop 'em. Let's go!"

And go they did, the horses cutting wide swaths in the long grass once they'd left that tangle of brush. A short time later they were climbing rising ground. Here the vegetation gave way to gravelly adobe earth. Farther on the ground was blanketed with loose chunks of rock, necessitating a careful picking of the way on the part of the shrewd cow ponies. Then a long rocky slope lay ahead. The horses were forced to a slow pace climbing this incline which eventually led them to the trail that ran toward Phantom Pass. Then once more the riders found level going.

Fifty yards ahead was the old adobe house. Lights still shone through its square, unpaned windows. Tanner called back, "Bud! You and George drop behind and see who's at the house. Don't be stingy with your lead if there's any call to use it!"

The other six riders forged ahead, swept past the house. At the entrance to the canyon, showing the way to Phantom Pass, the hoofs of the ponies struck sparks from the rough trail over which they passed.

Nogales was riding low on his pony's neck, with Caliper and Tanner on either side of him, the other three punchers close behind. It was difficult to make himself heard through the rush of wind, creaking of leather saddles and staccato pounding of hoofs, but Nogales finally got Tanner's attention.

"I'll go on ahead," he yelled, "and try to come up with the men near the front of the herd by the time the rest of you tackle the flank and tail riders."

The next instant the horsemen swept between two tall spires of rock that stood sentinel-like at the entrance to Phantom Pass. The pass had few turns but was fairly narrow in spots, and its floor was strewn with broken bits of rock. On either side steep granite walls rose precipitously from the level and towered high above their heads.

By this time Nogales was well in advance of his companions. Rounding a bend, he saw the herd and accompanying riders some short distance ahead. One of the flank riders had dropped back to the rear with his brother rustlers. The lead rider had, by this time, joined the remaining flanker. Now the moon was directly overhead, flooding the canyon pass with white light.

The rustlers stiffened suddenly, as their ears caught the sound of drumming hoofs. Glancing back, they saw Nogales approaching swiftly. Their hands dropped to holsters. Tanner and his other men were still beyond the bend in the pass, out of view of the rustlers. Seeing only one rider bearing down on them, their suspicions were, for the moment, allayed. After all, it might be only some lone rider cutting through the canyon on his way to Old Mexico.

The fact was that Nogales closed in on them so swiftly, they had little time to think or formulate any plan of action. As he came thundering on, the men at the rear made haste to start herding the cattle toward one wall, in the hopes Nogales would ride right through.

Nogales flashed past the tail men like a meteor, dodging past two of the slower cattle with a careening swiftness that almost swept his sure-footed pony to the ground, then again tore on. Before he was halfway through the herd, the pony picking its way with un-erring speed, Tanner and the others appeared on the scene.

One of the rustlers Nogales had just passed swore suddenly and unleashed a shot at Nogales — missed — then turned to face the oncoming Maple-Leaf men. Nogales pounded on, passed two more rustlers. He glanced back in time to see their six-guns flash out. At the same instant he jerked to a stop and wheeled his pony, bringing his own weapon into play. Fire streamed from his right hand. One of the rustlers toppled from his horse.

Something struck Nogales' pony a tremendous smash on the right shoulder. The beast faltered and went down.

Pandemonium suddenly broke loose. There was a confused din of roaring .45s and cursing voices. The cattle bellowed with fright and started to run. The noise of the melée was magnified times over in the narrow confines of the canyon walls.

As his horse crashed to the floor of the pass, Nogales loosened his feet from stirrups and landed on one shoulder. Catlike he rolled over and over and came erect again. His gun had gone spinning from his hand. He looked up in time to see a rustler riding down on him, crouched low behind his horse's head. Nogales jerked back just far enough to avoid being struck by the horse, reached out and seized the rustler's left leg.

He felt himself snatched violently from the earth but held grimly on. The man in the saddle swore an oath and swung toward Nogales. Orange flame spurted from his six-shooter. Nogales felt the breeze of the bullet pass close to his face.

By this time he had a more secure hold on the fellow's leg as he was dragged alongside the running horse. For a moment he caught his feet, ran with the pony a few steps, then with the other hand reached up and seized the rider's shirt.

At that instant the horse swerved. The rider lost his balance and was flung from the saddle with Nogales still hanging on for dear life. As they flashed through the air Nogales flung his body sidewise and managed to land on top when they struck the earth. Over and over the two rolled, each fighting for a telling hold. The frightened horse, relieved of its double burden, came to a stop a few feet away.

Kicking, clawing, panting — Nogales and his opponent continued their struggle. Suddenly the fight came to an abrupt finish when the other man's head collided with a chunk of loose rock. He groaned and relaxed his hold. Wearily Nogales rose to his feet, looking down on the other. The man lay quiet with no movement.

"Whew!" Nogales puffed like a porpoise. "What a tough baby I picked for that little shindig."

By this time the noise of the firing had stopped. Caliper came running up. "You all right, pard?"

"I'm all right. Bumped up a mite, that's all."

Nogales searched the ground for his gun and within a few minutes found it. Caliper went to examine two forms stretched on the earth. One of them was the man Nogales had fought with. He was merely stunned and already had commenced an incoherent muttering. The other rustler examined by Caliper was dead.

Nogales found his pony, still down with a broken shoulder. There was nothing left except to put a bullet through its brain.

"I sure hate to do this, pony." Nogales spoke regretfully. Reluctantly he pulled trigger.

At the sound of the shot Tanner came riding up. "Did you get another?" he yelled.

"Nope, I just had to finish my pony — or rather your pony, Lee. He took a slug of lead. There was nothing else could be done. What did you boys do?"

"One coyote wiped out complete. Five prisoners, two of 'em wounded slightly but they can navigate. One of my boys is scratched a mite from a flying hunk of lead — Murray Cramm — but he's all right."

Nogales said, "There's two more sidewinders over there a few steps. Caliper just reported one of 'em dead; the other I tussled with until he hit his head on a rock. That will make one more prisoner to bring in."

Tanner said disgustedly, "These coyotes didn't put up much resistance once we'd started to bear down on 'em. The biggest trouble was holding those cattle when they started to roll their tails. Didn't you hear the fuss?"

"Me, I was too busy in a wrestling match to hear anything. Lost my gun and had to fight it out with my grab-hooks. That's the feller I was telling about, that got knocked out."

Tanner made his way to where Nogales' opponent of a short time before, was just climbing to his feet. Nogales followed and seized the fellow's arm.

Caliper said, "Do you know him, Lee?" when Tanner grunted suddenly in recognition.

"This is Ward Austen — Krouch's foreman," Tanner said. "If he gave you much of a fight, Nogales, it must have been frantic fear spurring him on. I never figured him as tough."

"Any rat will fight like hell when he's cornered," Nogales replied.

The other Maple-Leaf men commenced to arrive with prisoners now. The prisoners were tied into saddles. Just before a start was made Austen broke down and displayed a desire to tell everything he knew regarding Krouch's activities, in the hope of saving his own skin. The Maple-Leaf men listened in silence, though their lips tightened ominously from time to time.

Finally the men with their prisoners got started. Nogales caught up one of the dead rustlers' horses and climbed into the saddle. Tanner left two men to bring in the cattle; the rest accompanied the captive rustlers. The horses moved out of the canyon, once more headed for the Maple-Leaf.

At the old adobe house a stop was made to pick up the two punchers Tanner had left behind. Here two more prisoners were found. George Tilden and Bud Thompson hadn't encountered any trouble in seizing their captives. Stan Cox, with two broken arms, had offered no resistance; the Circle-Slash cook hadn't shown any fight, either, claiming he had been hired to cook, not to handle a six-shooter.

Sometime later the Maple-Leaf riders herded their prisoners into Tanner's place and found Deputy Burgett there to take charge of the captured men. The story of the fight at Phantom Pass was quickly related to Burgett, then Nogales said, "There's a nest of sidewinders for you to take back to Orejano's jail, Burgett. How many of us do you want to accompany you with 'em?"

Burgett looked dubiously at the trussed-up rustlers. "I don't know," he said, "as we'd better take these skunks to my jail or not. It's old, none too solid. They might have friends in town. I wouldn't want a jail break pulled off. I'd like to see 'em put behind bars that are plumb solid —"

Nogales nodded. "What you say fits in with something that just came to mind. If Lee hasn't objections, I'd like to see these prisoners kept here for a day or so. There's no use of letting Krouch know his crew is being held captive by us for a short spell. Later we can take 'em to Arroyo City where there's a strong jail."

"That's smart," Tanner agreed. "We can keep these skunks down in the barn. I'll have a couple of boys keep watch on 'em day and night, until Burgett is ready to take 'em under armed guard to Arroyo City. We'll stick 'em in the barn right now."

"Wait a few minutes," Nogales said. "I'd like to question 'em a minute first. Austen broke down and spilled a lot of stuff to us regarding Krouch's game. Let's check his story with these boys' and get all the evidence possible."

"I agree with you." Tanner nodded. He glanced at the prisoners and could see from their faces that they were willing to tell anything possible that might aid them when it came time for their trial.

Nogales sized the men up, then said, "All right you cow-thieving galoots, who's first to make his little speech? Just remember that confession is good for the soul and that the more stuff you can lay at Straub Krouch's door, the lighter your own sentences will be —"

"I'll talk! I'll talk!" "I want to confess!" Several of the prisoners burst out.

Nogales laughed shortly. "You're sure eager to orate. All right, talk and talk fast. It's late and I don't crave to miss any more sleep than necessary. Max," to Deputy Burgett, "grab a pencil and paper and make notes. We're on the road to winding up Krouch's dirty plans for all time, and there's no time like the present for getting the evidence black on white!"

23. Roaring .45s

When the train arrived from Arroyo City the following afternoon, Nogales was on hand to meet it. One passenger alighted — Straub Krouch. In his hand he carried a small, well-packed canvas satchel.

All the ride back from Arroyo City Krouch had been indulging in daydreams regarding the millions to be made from oil lands and making rosy plans for the future. Why, in a year or so more he'd be a king in this country. Nothing could stop him now!

Consequently, Krouch was in a jovial mood when he stepped from the train, which barely paused to let him off before going on again. Krouch saw Nogales standing on the depot platform.

"Hello, Anderson," he greeted, pretending friendship, "how's tricks?"

Nogales ignored the outstretched hand. "Dammit," he growled, glancing around uneasily, "I told you not to use that Anderson name. Do you want somebody to hear you and pop me off for that reward?"

Krouch guffawed. "Aw, what's in a name?"

"You call me one and you'll find out," Nogales snapped. "Did you get the money?"

"Certainly I got it. Don't I always get anything I go after? I got it right here," lifting the canvas satchel in his hand. "Didn't have any trouble a-tall raising it. You see, the Circle-Slash and the Apache are both paying properties, and the bank was willing to loan money on 'em. While I was in Arroyo City I looked up title to the Star-M. It's all clear. All I've got to do is pay over the cash and get the bill of sale. I reckon to take you out with me to witness the deal —"

"What did you think I met you for?" Nogales growled. "I aim to watch every move you make, until half the Star-M is in my name —"

"Cripes! You don't have to be so suspicious. I'll be square with you. Let's get a drink."

"There you go," Nogales exclaimed angrily, "always putting pleasure before business. Let's get this Star-M business settled before somebody holds you up and steals that money —"

"Humph!" Krouch snorted scornfully. He threw back his coat and gestured toward his Colt guns, swung at hips. "Nobody's going to hold up Straub Krouch while he's wearing these two protectors. Besides, what's the hurry? I've got a two-day option."

"Hang your option! In the first place, options aren't worth a hoot in hell sometimes, when you're competing against big organizations. In the second place" — Nogales paused impressively — "that representative of the Southwest Cattle Company was out to the Star-M this noon. Fact is he stayed for dinner, and he and Lena Lou were right friendly."

"No!" Krouch turned pale. "What happened, do you know?"

Nogales shrugged his shoulders. "I'll tell you this much — I don't know how much impression the feller made on Lena Lou, but he was hinting around that it was too bad she couldn't get more than forty thousand for her place —"

"What were you doing there?" Krouch asked.

"I'd gone out to get my gear. I was talking to Caliper, too. They asked me to eat, so naturally I stayed. Lena Lou told the cattle company man she'd given you a two-day option. Said if the money wasn't in her hand by the time the option expired, the whole deal would be off."

Krouch grew excited. "Hell's bells! We'd better get out there *pronto!* Come on, I'll get my horse —"

"Your bronc is all saddled, waiting for you at the Apache," Nogales replied. "I took care of that for you. Figured you'd be honing to move. I didn't aim to see you held back. There's too much at stake, and I'm interested in this deal as much as you are. The sooner

I leave Orejano, the better."

"I can believe that, Anderson," Krouch sneered.

"Cut it out, Krouch."

"Oh, all right. No need to go on the prod. Is Burgett in town?"

"He wasn't in his office when I looked in half an hour ago," Nogales replied truthfully.

Krouch grinned nastily. "Maybe he's still following that trail you left when you pulled out in such a hurry yesterday."

Nogales shrugged. "*Quién sabe?* I don't know and I don't care. I don't intend to be pushed around by law officers, I do know that."

Grudging admiration showed in Krouch's eyes when he answered, "You may be a damn fool, Anderson, but I'll say one thing for you — you got guts."

"Say, do you have to talk all the time?" Nogales growled. By this time they were abreast of the Apache Saloon tie rail. "Come on, here's your horse. Let's ride!"

Krouch climbed into his saddle. Then, with the satchel of money held before him, he spurred out of Orejano, Nogales close at his side.

The ride to the Star-M was made in fast time, Nogales leading the way after they'd passed the town limits and refusing all attempts to indulge in conversation. He replied only once when Krouch shouted to him through the rush of wind, "How soon can you get me your twenty thousand?"

"Just the minute you make out papers giving me a half share in the Star-M," Nogales yelled back, "providing everything goes to your satisfaction."

Krouch looked surprised. "You got the money with you?"

This time Nogales didn't answer except to nod shortly.

Krouch's jaw dropped slightly, his eyes widened. He started to say something else, but Nogales spurred ahead of him at the moment. Krouch rode on, making plans. After all, an ounce of lead would be a small price in return for twenty thousand dollars!

There was no one in sight at the Star-M when the two men rode into the ranch yard. However, as they dismounted from their horses, Lena Lou appeared at the back door. Old Pablo stood just behind her.

Lena Lou nodded quietly to Nogales, then turned to Krouch. "So you did come back, *Mister* Krouch. I never expected to see you again."

Krouch laughed shortly. "Certain I come back. I've got the money right here. You won't own the Star-M much longer."

Lena Lou frowned. Even now she didn't understand. Nogales had warned Caliper and Tanner not to explain matters to her. All she knew was that Straub Krouch was paying an unheard-of price for her run-down ranch. She stood aside to let Nogales and Krouch enter the kitchen, which was a large room with a stove at one side. Other furniture consisted of a cupboard, two straight-backed chairs and a table.

"I've got the deed here," Lena Lou said. "The papers are all drawn up, ready for signatures. It's going to take me a little time to pack the things I want, but I figure you can take over the Star-M one week from today."

"That suits me." Krouch nodded. He placed his satchel on a chair, opened it. "Here's the money. I suppose you'll want to count it."

"You suppose correctly," Lena Lou stated tartly, "on any money I receive from you. Pablo and I" — she smiled coldly — "may even bite some of the coins just to make sure they're not counterfeit —"

"You're too hard on me, Lena Lou," Krouch growled, looking ugly.

"I couldn't be," Lena Lou snapped.

While she was counting out the money, Krouch was looking over the papers, deed and so on. Everything was found to be in good order; he could find nothing about which to kick. Lena Lou finished counting the gold, silver and bills at last, placing the money on the table in small piles as she worked. Then she signed the bill of sale, which was witnessed by Nogales and Pablo.

Krouch grunted with satisfaction as he tucked the bill of sale into his pocket. Lena Lou had produced a small canvas sack and was starting to scoop her piles of cash money into it. She stopped once, looking up to face Krouch, who was still standing there, watching her.

"That closes the deal, doesn't it, Krouch?" she asked in chilly accents.

"Not quite," Krouch commenced easily. "I —"

"Now what do you want?" Lena Lou paused and replaced on the table a package of greenbacks she'd been about to drop in her canvas sack. "Just because you've bought the Star-M is no sign my feelings toward you are changed. You can take over the property one week from today. Until then the Star-M is mine. Good day, *Mister* Krouch!"

Abruptly Straub Krouch's manner changed: his hands darted to hips and came up holding leveled six-shooters. An expression of snarling hate crossed his coarse features.

"Don't be in such a hurry to make off with that money," he growled. "You, Nogales — Pablo — reach for the ceiling — stick 'em high! Keep back, gal — don't try to reach your gun on that wall there. Reach, blast you!"

"Hey, what's the idea?" Nogales exclaimed angrily.

Lena Lou stood at one side of the room,

her hands above her head, near Pablo, who had elevated his arms. Nogales stood apart from the two, his hands also held high. Slowly the three backed from the menacing muzzles of Krouch's Colt guns.

"Get back there!" Krouch ordered. "Don't try nothing funny —"

"What do you think you're doing?" Nogales snapped.

"I don't *think*." Krouch grinned evilly. "I'm doing it!" His brain was working swiftly. He might let Nogales in on his plan and then later take the cowboy's twenty thousand. No, it was best to make a clean sweep now. Nogales could go out with the others. Krouch's nasty laugh sounded through the room. "Thought I was a fool, didn't you? Do you think I'm going to let a gal get away with that much of my money? You've got another guess coming. I've the bill of sale for the Star-M. Now I aim to get back the money I paid for it — get back there! You three keep your hands high!"

Nogales paused in mid-stride and stiffened his arms again. "You're plumb simple, Krouch, if you think you can steal back that money. You'd have to leave the country. You wouldn't have the Star-M or your Circle-Slash, either. You can't —"

"Oh, can't I?" Krouch snarled, thumbs hooked over his drawn-back gun hammers, the muzzles of which moved continually to

285

keep all three within range of his aim. "It will only need three chunks of hot lead to settle for you and the gal and that old greaser. I figure three ca'tridges is a right cheap price to pay. There's nobody around here but us four. It'll be one of those mystery killings that never get solved. And, *Red Anderson*, you can start emptying your pockets of that twenty thousand dollars. You've been asking me when I wanted it. I want it now!"

"You beast!" Lena Lou exclaimed. "You never intended to play square with us —"

"Depends on what you mean by square." Krouch smiled nastily. "I play square with Straub Krouch — nobody else. And I planned it well. I'll have the money and the Star-M oil lands both —"

"Oil lands?" Lena Lou exclaimed, looking puzzled. "There's no oil on my holdings."

"No, Lena Lou," Nogales said quietly, "there isn't — but Krouch thinks there is." A small wooden chair stood at Nogales' side. Now he moved one foot nearer a leg of the chair while he continued: "I didn't tell you about the oil-lands business before because I was afraid you'd look on the deal as a deception. But in Krouch's case you have to fight fire with fire, and I added a mite of oil to the flames to make it burn brighter — though even then Krouch was too dumb to see through it —"

There burst from Krouch's throat an animal-like howl of rage. "Damn you, Nogales! Have you double-crossed me?"

"No," Nogales said steadily, "I didn't double-cross you. Your own imagination did that. You jumped to conclusions —"

"By the livin' Gawd, you tricked me!" Krouch bawled, tilting his guns ominously.

Nogales said grimly, "You got no more than the murderer of Lena Lou's father deserved, Straub Krouch —"

He had no time to say more. A murderous gleam had entered Krouch's small eyes. His fingers were quivering about six-shooter triggers.

And at that instant Nogales went into action. His toe shot forward to hook a rung of the chair at his right. The chair was abruptly jerked from the floor to go hurtling through the air in the direction of Krouch's head. Krouch tried to duck the flying chair. At the same instant his guns roared!

White spurts of flame darted from Nogales' gun, as Krouch's bullets ripped harmlessly into the ceiling. Krouch had staggered back under the chair and then leaped to one side to unleash further shots. At that instant Nogales' bullet struck him and whirled him around. Again Nogales fired.

Krouch went crashing into the table, overturning it and sending the piles of money flying in all directions across the floor. For an instant, shielded behind the overturned table, he paused, then struggling to right himself, stumbled over one leg of the table and sprawled in an ungainly heap as his six-shooters dropped from his hands.

The next instant the door to the adjoining room burst open, and Caliper, followed by Lee Tanner, came rushing into the kitchen.

"We couldn't wait any longer," Caliper exclaimed. "I had Krouch covered through a crack in the door, and Tanner was all for interfering before, but I told him Nogales could handle the situation."

Krouch was the only one in the room who hadn't known of the two secreted beyond that door.

Nogales bent over Krouch and examined him. The man's eyes were closed but he was conscious. Blood was slowly seeping into his shirt. He moaned feebly. Nogales spoke his name. Krouch's eyelids fluttered then opened.

Nogales said gravely, "You'll be leaving here right soon, Krouch. Don't you want to make a statement first? The ghost herd is busted up. We caught Austen and the others last night — got the names of certain confederates you've had working with you from time to time. They're all to be rounded up. Austen and your punchers confessed. They lay the murder of Lena Lou's father at your door —"

"It's a lie, it's a lie," Krouch groaned. "I never done it —"

"Think carefully, Krouch," Nogales urged. "You'll want a clear conscience where you're going — don't you think you'd better come clean?"

Stark terror showed in Krouch's eyes. A moan parted his lips. "All right — all right," he quavered. "I want to get right with everybody before I die. I own up. It's my gang that has been doing all the rustling. I shot Lena Lou's father. I wanted the Star-M — figured she'd be easy to beat down to terms. I guess I was crazy for power."

Nogales laughed and rose to his feet. "Well, that's that," he said briskly. "You all heard that confession — just in case he should get reluctant about repeating it to the judge —"

"Isn't Krouch dying?" Caliper asked in surprise.

"Where did you ever get that idea?" Nogales grinned. "Don't let a little blood fool you, pard. You should know my shooting better than that. Killing would be too easy for him. All he's got is a couple of smashed shoulders. It was shock and fright that knocked him out."

"But I heard you say he was going to leave here," Tanner said, "right soon."

"He is," Nogales chuckled, "on his way to prison."

Krouch had heard the words in dismay. Now he struggled to his feet, eyes blazing with hate, pain and unholy rage. "Damn you, Nogales," he screamed. "You've double-crossed me at every turn. But I'll fix you. I'll tell the authorities where Red Anderson can be found —"

Nogales shook his head. "Red Anderson was captured and hung quite a spell back, Krouch. Your imagination played you dirt there, too, as well as on oil lands."

Krouch stood swaying before him, almost frothing at the mouth. "You've swindled me out of money on this Star-M deal. That deal won't hold — misrepresentation of facts —" So great was his fury he was unable to continue.

"There was nothing about oil represented by the owner," Nogales said sternly. "It was your own greedy mind that fooled you. The deal stands. You can raise your trial-defense money on the Star-M maybe — but I don't reckon it will do you any good. We've got you dead to rights!" Nogales turned to Pablo. "Take this buzzard down to the bunkhouse and fix him so he won't bleed to death. Burgett should be along to take him into custody in a short while, then he and his rustling crew can all head for Arroyo City and jail at the same time. And I aim to see that a strong guard of cow hands makes the trip with 'em."

Pablo nodded and helped the still-cursing Krouch through the kitchen door. Nogales followed them to the doorway and stood looking after them until they turned into the bunkhouse. He gave a long, satisfied sigh. "I reckon this country will be plumb peaceful now," he said quietly.

24. Lena Lou Picks Her Man

Meanwhile the others in the kitchen were helping Lena Lou retrieve her scattered money from the floor and stuffing it into the canvas sack she held. Nogales turned back into the room and stood watching them, a smile on his face.

Lena Lou said soberly, "I almost feel as if I'd cheated Krouch out of this money."

"Don't you feel thataway, Lena Lou," Nogales said quickly. "Krouch was out to cheat you. Think of the Star-M cattle he's stolen and — and —" He paused, not wanting to bring back memories of the girl's murdered father, then, "Why, that price would be about right, if your cattle went with it. Look at it that way. Krouch is just paying now for something he should have paid for long ago."

"I know, you're right," she admitted, sensing what had prompted the hesitation in his words. "I suppose I should be glad the deal has gone through — glad and thankful to you — but, somehow, I'm going to hate to leave the old place. It's been home for so many years."

Caliper put in, "Ten to one you can buy it back from Krouch for a heap less money than he paid: He's going to need money bad for his trial — though I figure it won't do him any good."

Lena Lou nodded, then turned to Tanner. "Don't you think it's about time we told them, Lee?"

Tanner grinned. "The sooner the better."

The girl swung back to face Nogales and Caliper. "Some time ago Lee asked me to marry him. I said I wouldn't, unless the time came when I could bring him something more than the added worry of the Star-M. Now the wedding needn't be postponed any longer, with everything settled. And that's something else Lee and I have to thank you two for."

To Nogales and Caliper the announcement came with all the stunning force of an exploding bomb. Their faces were blank with dismay, uncomprehending. For a few moments neither could speak.

Nogales recovered himself first. "Con— congratulations, Lena Lou," he stammered, forcing a sickly smile.

The girl looked sharply at him. "What's wrong? Do you feel ill?"

Nogales gulped and shook his head. "It's just the smell of gunpowder lingering in the room," he said bravely. "It always sort of upsets my system. It'll pass in a minute."

Now Caliper found his voice. "You dang muddlewitted rannie," he said impatiently, "don't you know any etiquette? It's always the man that gets congratulated. The girl just gets wished good luck." He turned to Tanner and extended one hand. "And I know she won't have to worry about that, Lee."

Tanner said thanks and shook hands with both men as did Lena Lou.

By this time Nogales was commencing to feel himself again. "Caliper and I could see how the land lay between you two," he fabricated. "We could see what was coming —"

"We sure could." Caliper also proved himself an able liar. "Why, it was only last night, when we were waiting on the hogback, that Nogales and I were talking about you two getting hitched up. We were trying to decide what to give you for a wedding present. Wasn't we, Nogales?"

Nogales nodded vigorously. "Yes, we sure were. And we decided that a third interest in the Maple-Leaf would be plumb appropriate. Lee has already put in money leasing the property, and I figure he should get some return, anyway —"

"Heck." Tanner looked his bewilderment. "The Maple-Leaf," he stammered, "is owned by the Southwest Cattle Company —"

"That's us," Nogales grinned.

"Nogales being the cattle and me the company," Caliper put in with a chuckle.

"You see," Nogales explained, "last spring I fell heir to a lot of property and money, the

Maple-Leaf being part of the property, along with a heap of other odds and ends. I was for taking it easy, but Caliper, being dumb, insists on working. He's independent thataway. So we arranges between us for him to be the manager of the Maple-Leaf, him knowing cattle breeding like he does — in fact he doesn't know anything else. Anyway, for his work he was to get a one-third share in the outfit. He can't back out of that, because I've got legal papers to prove it. We came down here to take charge and found you here. Lee, you've proved yourself. You go ahead and do the work, while Caliper and I roam around the country some more."

"Why, Nogales — Caliper — Lee — !" Lena Lou exclaimed, unable to say more.

"Well I'll be danged," Tanner burst out. "Say, it's a wonder that Southwest Cattle Company lawyer didn't mention anything about Caliper being the manager when I signed the lease for the ranch. Why do you suppose that was?"

"Shucks," Nogales snickered, "he didn't know anything about it. He thought he was doing business for me. Caliper and I didn't make our agreement until after we'd left him. It doesn't make any difference, anyway. That law sharp doesn't know anything about cows."

Tanner was finally convinced after some further explanations.

"What are you going to do now?" Lena Lou asked, after she and Tanner had thanked the two. "I should think, with all that money, you two would find yourselves a couple of nice girls, get married and settle down on one of your many properties. I'll bet there are plenty of nice girls in this country would be glad to find husbands —"

"Huh!" Caliper started nervously, then wagged his head emphatically. "No sirree! Marriage is all right for some folks but not for Nogales and me. We aim to be free so we can pick up and amble around the country any time the notion strikes us. Getting married is one thing that never did occur to us, did it, Nogales?"

Nogales spoke with scornful astonishment. "What, us! *Get married?* You and me? I — should — say — not! That's something to which we never did give a serious thought —"

And, as a matter of fact, they really hadn't.

About the Author

(*Allan*) *William Colt MacDonald* was born in Detroit, Michigan in 1891. His formal education concluded after his first three months of high school when he went to work as a lathe operator for Dodge Brothers' Motor Company. His first commercial writing consisted of advertising copy and articles for trade publications. While working in the advertising industry, MacDonald began contributing stories of varying lengths to pulp magazines and his first novel, a Western story, was published by Clayton House in *Ace-high Magazine* in 1925. MacDonald later commented that when this first novel appeared in book form as *Restless Guns* in 1929, "I quit my job cold." From the time of that decision on, MacDonald's career became a long string of successes in pulp magazines, hardcover books, films, and eventually original and reprint paperback editions. The Three Mesquiteers, MacDonald's most famous characters, were introduced in 1933 in *Law of the Forty-fives*. His other most famous character creation was Gregory Quist, a railroad detective. Some of MacDonald's finest work occurs outside his series, especially the well researched *Stir Up The Dust* which was published first in a British edition in 1950 and *The Mad Marshal* in 1958. MacDonald's only son, Wallace, recalled how much fun his father had writing Western fiction. It is an apt observation since countless readers have enjoyed his stories now for nearly three quarters of a century.

The employees of Thorndike Press hope you have enjoyed this Large Print book. All our Thorndike and Wheeler Large Print titles are designed for easy reading, and all our books are made to last. Other Thorndike Press Large Print books are available at your library, through selected bookstores, or directly from us.

For information about titles, please call:

(800) 223-1244

or visit our Web site at:

www.gale.com/thorndike
www.gale.com/wheeler

To share your comments, please write:

Publisher
Thorndike Press
295 Kennedy Memorial Drive
Waterville, ME   04901